# THE EGREGIOUS AFFAIR OF A COLD-HEARTED KING

AF583231

KAYLIANI SHI

This book is a work of fiction. Names, characters, places, and incidents are the products of the author's imagination or are used fictitiously. Any resemblance to actual events, locales, or persons, living or dead, is coincidental.

Copyright © 2026 Kayliani Shi, Candescent Ink Press

Interior Design by Kayliani Shi

Cover Design by Kayliani Shi

Map Design by Marta Riva

Cover copyright © 2026 by Candescent Ink Press.

The scanning, uploading, and distribution of this book or parts of this book without permission is a theft of the author's intellectual property. If you would like permission to use material from the book (other than for review purposes), please contact thekaylianishireadsbooks@gmail.com.

Thank you for your support of the author's rights.

First Edition: July 2026

Candescent Ink Press

Candescent Ink Press is an LLC established and owned by Kayliani Shi. It serves as a self-publishing imprint. Candescent Ink Press books may be purchased in bulk for business, educational, or promotional use. For information, please contact your local bookseller and direct them to the Ingram site.

Library of Congress Control Number: 2026914913

ISBN: 979-8-234-00719-3 (Paperback)

Dear reader,

This prequel is part of *The Shadowed Throne* duology. It is intended to be read **after** *The Sinuous Bargain of a Cowardly Prince* and before book two. Reading it before book one will spoil major plot points and mysteries presented in book one.

## Content Warning

This work contains depictions of fantasy violence and references to sexual assault (fade-to-black, not depicted on page). It explores trauma, power imbalance, and obsession. It is not a romance. Mild language is also present. Please take care while reading and prioritize your comfort.

***The Shadowed Throne Chronicles***

*Reading Order*

***Book 1:*** *The Sinuous Bargain of a Cowardly Prince*
***Book 1.5:*** *The Egregious Affair of a Cold-Hearted King*
***Book 2:*** *The Unyielding Heir of a Cursed Kingdom*

The Valley
Perri Duchy
Arioch's Castle
BellMane
Outer Villages
LouNym
The Kingdom of Arioch

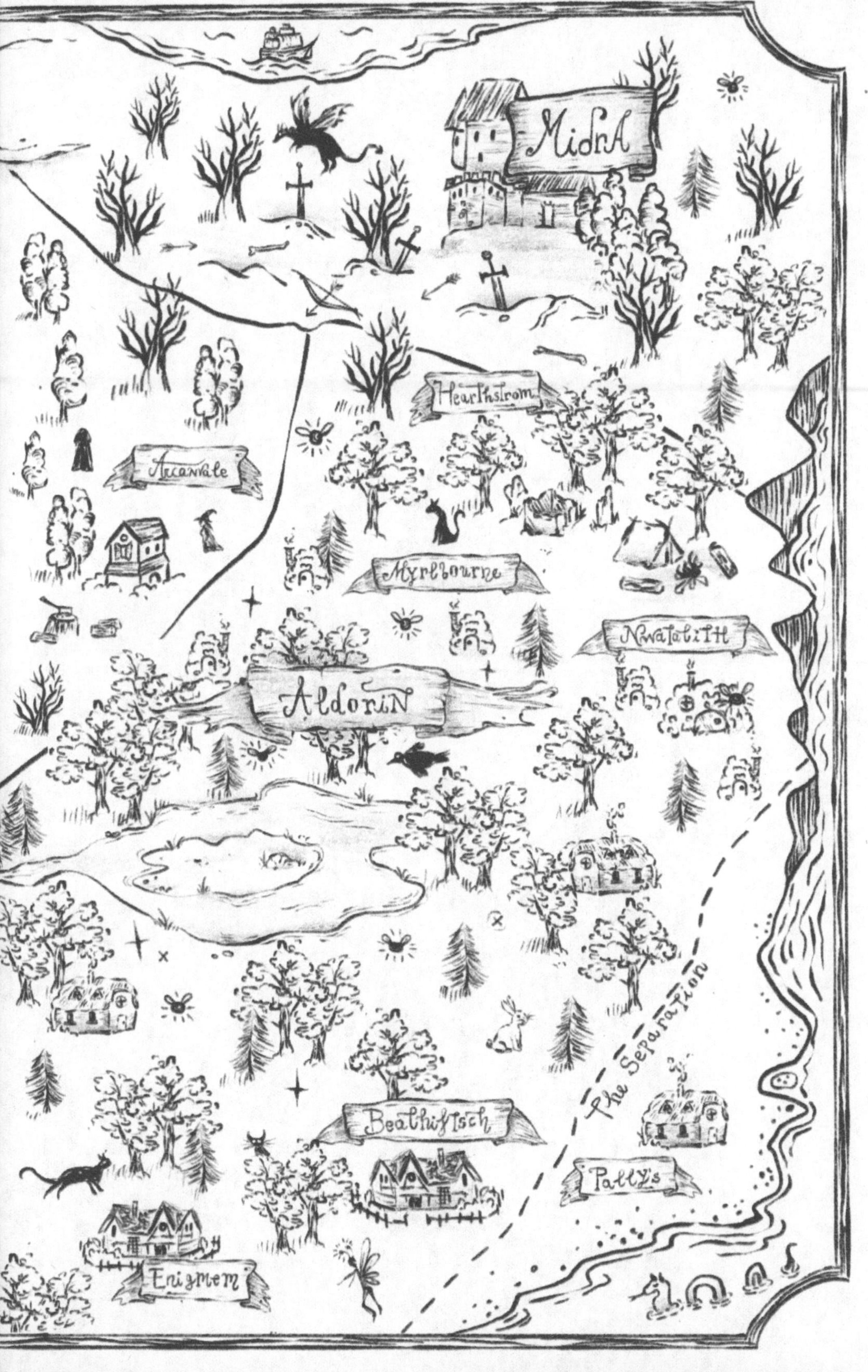
MidnA
Hearthstrom
Arcanvale
Myrlbourne
Nwatalith
Aldorin
Beathifisch
The Separation
Pally's
Enigmem

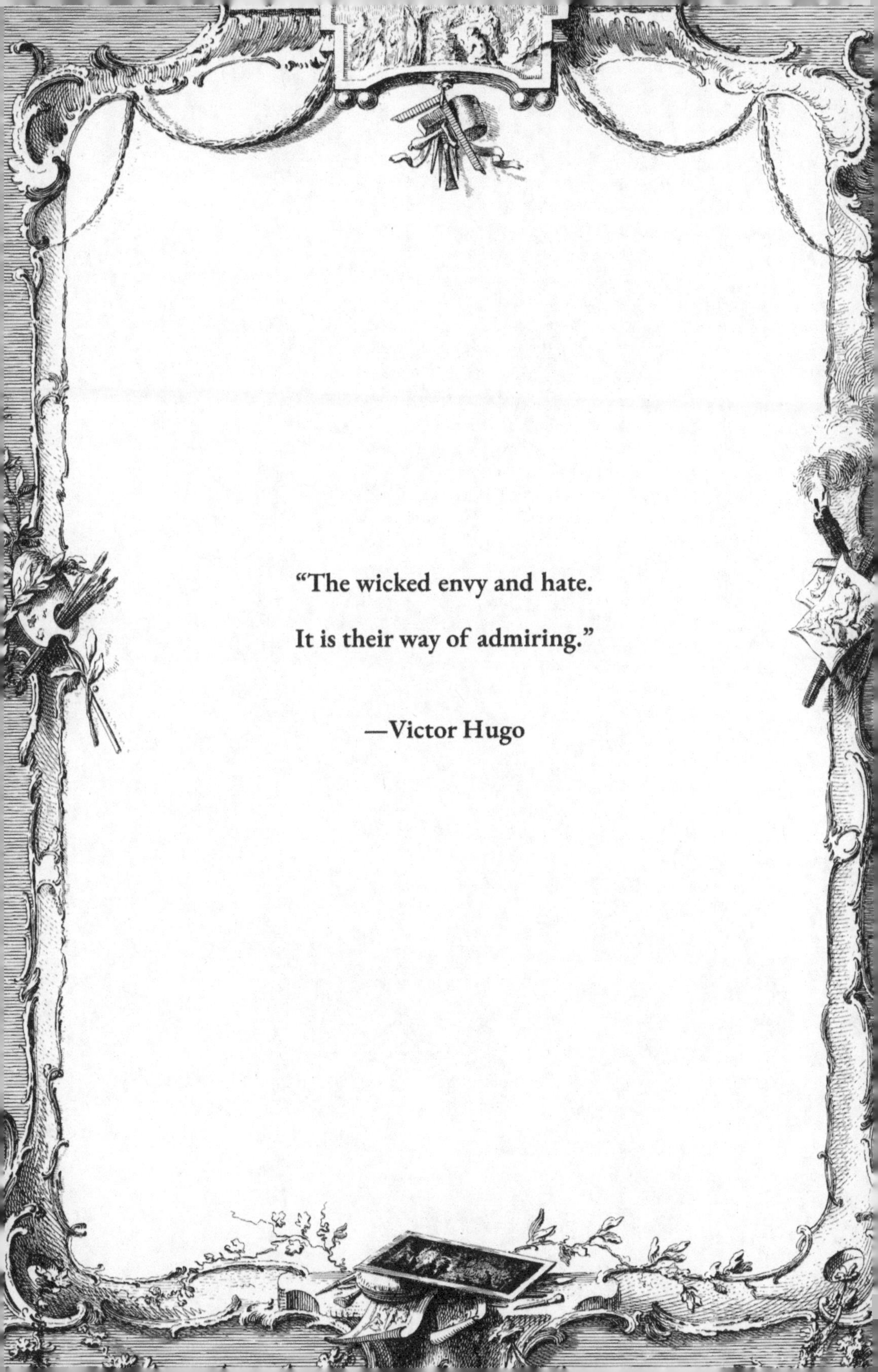

“The wicked envy and hate.

It is their way of admiring.”

—Victor Hugo

# PROLOGUE

## The War of Undying
### A MILLENNIUM BEFORE PRESENT DAY

The queen of Aldorin plunged her fingers into the rent flesh of a fallen soldier, keen on removing the poison-tipped arrow burrowed there. Black blood oozed over her hands as she retrieved the bolt. The elf soldier stared up at her, his eyes blank and glassy. With her clean hand, the elf queen gently drew them shut.

A tear arched to her chin. It wasn't the first to fall that day, and it wouldn't be the last.

Her people were quickly losing this war—they were outnumbered, not by the humans they faced, but by the beasts and creatures fighting alongside the mortals. The dragons, once loyal to the goddess Aldorin and highly revered by all, now sliced through anyone blocking the path of the tyrant king, Arioch Faundor. Their eyes, which once held such depth and divinity, were now crazed with a nightmarish sheen... Darkness poisoned their discernment, its venom eased only by blind obedience to their human masters.

The queen drew in a shuddering breath and raised the silver-tipped arrowhead with her thin fingers. The weapon glistened under the glaring sun as she tilted it back and forth. Though speckled with blood, the metal still reflected her immortal beauty. A beauty that cursed her, made her an object of desire.

Liquid ebony hair flowed around her, and her long, sharp-tipped ears protruded elegantly between the wild strands of obsidian. She'd been Arioch's coveted creature since he'd come to conquer their lands—more than her beauty, he wished to claim her power as his own. When she'd refused to give herself to him, he didn't hesitate to bleed her land dry, threaten her people, and force a war upon them.

Death cries filled the air, but they were muffled beneath the deafening roars of bloodthirsty warlords, keen on relishing their kills while her people shrieked, fighting until their very last breath.

All to no avail.

The queen dropped the arrowhead into the dead grass and rose to her feet, standing tall in her thin black gown. She was no fighter—she preferred to heal and care for the injured. Elven magic was pure, sanctified, which meant it was impossible for it to be used for any evil act—including taking another's life. Her heavenly mother Aldorin dictated this pure use of magic. But the queen's people were dying by the dozens, and though she was blessed with immortality and magic abilities beyond that of normal elves, not even *she* could revive the dead.

"Nadia!"

Her ears twitched as she turned her attention to the scrawny, winged creature dodging the slashing of blades on his way to her.

"Elias." Nadia lifted an eyebrow when he stopped before her. He bowed and she returned it. "Our people are dying. Why are you coming to me now when we rely on your battle prowess to win this war?"

The fairy king was breathless as he hovered there, wings

lowering him to the ground. The emptiness in his gray eyes told her everything she needed to know—whatever words he spoke would damn them.

"We've been cornered, my queen. The humans shouldn't have stood a chance, but... This magic they possess is just—"

A scream ripped through Nadia's left ear. Another one of her men had been speared. She and Elias helplessly beheld the soldier —he teetered on unstable knees, arms outstretched to maintain his balance. The light of life still glistened in his dark green eyes, just barely.

*He is still savable,* Nadia thought.

She rushed to the soldier. The fairy king followed closely behind. Around them, the stretch of flat grassland was filled with bodies twisting and contorting against iron and steel, the shrieks and grunts of men and women violently ripping through the air.

The soldier sucked in a wheezy breath when Nadia knelt next to him. The damp, muddy ground seeped through the soft fabric of her dress, and she averted her eyes from the wound blooming within his abdomen.

Though she was no warrior, she knew how to bring light and healing like no other. The lifeblood of the goddess Aldorin ran thick in her veins, and *it* was what gave her purpose. Whereas human royalty came with embellishments, political leverage, and war, elves turned to her as a figure to behold and respect. A conduit for her heavenly mother.

Their queen.

She could not fail yet another one of her people.

"What is your name?" She placed her hand in his, feeling for the pulse along his wrist.

"Beuton." He coughed. "Qor Beuton."

Nadia smiled as she lowered him gently into the dirt and cleared a few stones where his head would lay.

"You have a name *kings* would envy, Qor." The queen visually assessed his wounds. Her hand gently brushed along the side of the soldier's dirt-stained face, tracing his square jawline with her knuckles. "Can you promise me something? Don't let them know you're alive. Stay here until the enemy retreats."

He smiled at her, his lids heavy.

"Nadia." Urgency twanged in Elias's voice. "This soldier will meet death soon. Unless you want all of this to be for nought, we must run. *Now.*"

The elf queen's jaw tightened. She did not look at the fairy king; instead, she swept her blotchy hand over the death wound, willing her endless magical energy into her fingers. Warmth stretched from within her chest and expanded outward to her hand, where it tingled for a second before a glowing ball of light manifested from her fingertips. She lowered the healing magic into the wound, watching with relief as the wound sealed itself and smoothed the breath of the soldier.

They were losing, but at least *one* of her soldiers would live to tell the tale.

Finally, Nadia turned to the fairy king, whose small, wretched face was laced with concern.

"We will not run. Not after we've lost so many." Nadia's eyebrows tightened.

"My queen, you do not understand. That is the reason why we must leave. Now. Or *all* of our people will—"

The sharp, jagged claws of a dragon plunged through the fairy's chest from behind, grabbing the poor creature's heart and tearing it out through his back. His torso collapsed in on itself—a mess of skin and bones and gore, and he fell to the ground, lifeless. The words he didn't speak were overcome by Nadia's scream.

She scrambled up, her palms skidding on gore. The world tilted, turning the gray sun into a hot, white smear.

What the fairy king said had been true all along: they were suffering a devastating defeat. Hope had long since left them.

The dragon seemed to watch her as it indulged in the meaty heart of her closest ally, licking the blood dripping from its jagged teeth. Bile rose to her throat. She swallowed it and turned her back to the beast.

This had all happened because of her. Had she surrendered long ago, would the outcome be any different? She knew Arioch was drunk on control, on power. He wouldn't stop until he had every potential threat bent and molded around his fingers.

It seemed terribly pointless to surrender now. Had he expected she would eventually? After breaking her, after showing her the power he already possessed?

She looked around hopelessly at the bodies piled atop one another. Not a single one of her soldiers had survived, save for Qor, who played dead among his friends.

Her cheeks had grown wet with mourning, but she forced herself to stand. As she walked among the carnage, her bare feet nearly slipped on the many sweaty, bloodied limbs littering the field.

Though Nadia was physically small and weak, her heavenly mother's magic kept her alive. This allowed her to care for her people, to teach them the ways of magic. Through her, all elves could become one with the forest she'd grown so fond of. But even with her endless existence, Nadia was not invulnerable, especially not to the overwhelming tragedy thrumming in her veins like a poison.

Her knees gave out beneath her. The warm and sticky residue that caught her both horrified and calmed her. All at once, she wished she had fallen on an erect blade so her own lifeblood would join that of her soldiers. If she were to pass away, her people would despair, but at least the cruel human king couldn't steal her or the pure magic she possessed. She could never take her own life, though, no matter how desperately she might wish it; this was her curse.

She would forever despise Aldorin for bestowing her with it.

The fairy-slaying dragon flapped its wings as it hovered above her, claws slick with Elias's lifeblood. She glanced up, then realized with a newfound terror that the monster wasn't wild—it had a rider whose silhouette masked the gray sun.

The dragon's large, thick limbs rumbled the earth and its master slid from a large saddle clasped under its breastbone. The man's face was dark and cold, speckled with red facial hair. His eyes were black as voids and his skin was scarred and bruised from battle. He was not immortal, but the glint of his grin proved he was the farthest thing from human.

Turning to face the light, King Arioch's sneer was like the waning moon and his eyes enviously reflected the power he saw in her. He lifted her with a thick, muscly arm, and secured her to his waist. He clamped a hand over her mouth so she couldn't scream when he slit her palm and collected the blood in a cloudy vial. Then he removed her from his hip and flung her onto the dragon's spiny back.

Her body was limp. She could not move, no matter how she tried. It was as though her limbs had given up, given into despair, and decided surrender was the best option. Complete and utter submission to the man who slayed all of her soldiers, who'd somehow rallied the dragons to his side.

Nadia should have escaped when Elias gave her the chance. She should have run away, using her magic to conceal herself and the fairy king.

Why hadn't she?

Her people *lost.*

The fairy king *died*, all because of her weakness.

In the end, the human king got what he wanted.

What more could she do now?

Arioch secured her to the beast's saddle, paying no mind to the scales that punctured her supple skin, and forced the dragon into the air. They flew over the battlefield riddled with gore-covered men, and Nadia's heart plunked to the bottom of her stomach. Her eyes bled fresh tears, her chest heaved a sob. Great sadness rooted itself in the gaping hole in her heart.

She'd abandoned her people.

She couldn't save them.

She couldn't even save *herself*.

And now she'd have to pay the price.

For many years, Nadia lived without light.

The castle's dungeons bore no window for her to feel the hot rays of sun or smell the fresh breezes that came with the changing seasons. Nadia lacked both the courage and the shamelessness to escape, so she remained in the darkness, curled into a corner of her cold cell. In this silence, she decided she would pay for her sins. She would not send a single prayer to her heavenly mother above, whose judgment she feared.

If any of her people managed to escape, they would mark her as deceased, which to her was more than she deserved for her cowardice.

For twenty years, Nadia drew circles in the dust and tied knots in her dress. The guards at her cell paid her no mind.

The mortal king only visited her once before he perished, his angled face cruel and set with hatred. King Arioch had aged, his once-vibrant red hair now speckled with gray. He peered at her through the opening in the heavy oak door of her cell, smiling with that crooked moonlike grin. She understood then what he thought: *I captured the elven queen! She is powerless against me, and her power is mine at last!*

For the first time in her long life, Nadia's heart twisted with its first thorn of malice, sprouting from fear and anger at the king who'd imprisoned her. It was so subtle, she hardly noticed its appearance. Hardly noticed when it planted its seed within her.

She dragged her stiff body to the window in the door. The walls flickered behind the weak torch he gripped in a wrinkled hand. He beheld her with that grin, softened only slightly with age, and she would've thought it his resting expression if he hadn't frowned the second she closed the distance between them.

His voice cut through the silence.

"As is true of the Perri Dukes of old, your blood henceforth belongs to *me*. A pity it took me so long to decide how best to use it." His voice was brittle, edged with death, but his black eyes burned with the life the rest of his body had already surrendered. "The witch who gave me the curse was wicked indeed. She enchanted your blood, this was the part of the bargain we agreed on, but she twisted our fates against us, so each of my descendants may have only one chance to harness your power for his own."

Nadia stepped away from him, her stomach souring at the thought that the king would admit such cruelty to her. The witch's mercy upon her hardly crossed her mind. She remembered when her palm was slit and he'd collected the blood. It must have been for this rotten curse. When she met his gaze again, she saw he greatly enjoyed her anguish.

Arioch would be the first of many kings to abuse her power; he at once made her curse her own people, for their cunning military strategy was known to be the strongest in the land. She was forced to handicap them, to make it impossible for them to succeed against even the weakest adversary.

The curse was simple, yet Nadia gnashed her teeth when she was forced to command it. "Why must I live while countless die?"

It pained her to speak, the curse fighting to take her over. "What have my people done for them to deserve such contempt?"

The door slid open heavily and the king crept toward her, his body haggard with age but still imposing. With his free hand, he drove a knife through her palm. This time, the blade pierced through bone and sliced the skin protecting her knuckles.

He reveled at the pain in her eyes, at her shriek as dark blood spouted from her hand and glistened as it dripped to the ground. Even for a never-ending being like her, she could not withstand Arioch's twisted blade, less the cruel torment death dangled before her, just beyond her reach. He must have known she couldn't commit the act, herself, nor would he kill her.

Arioch pulled the knife out of her and the wound sewed itself together quickly, the divine magic in her veins preserving her.

The old king watched in fascination, greed filling his dark eyes.

Her blood was now his to control. The power in her conformed to the monarch's will, stiffening her body. The curse took its hold, the obedience in the king's previous command filling her with dread.

And so, the first curse—perverting her pure power—was cast from her trembling lips. Her people were to always tell the truth; if they did not, they would suffer consequences that, when left unchecked, could suffocate and even kill them.

The moment the curse was spoken, the queen knew she alone was immune to it. She decided to use this to her own advantage. She would use it to leave her cell. To find her people. To retaliate.

Her heart ached at the thought of leaving, not because she knew her escape was futile, but because she knew if she were to make it out of the dungeons and find her people, she wouldn't be able to reverse the curse she'd cast upon them. No curse could be removed, not even by the caster. It is how the ruler of the seven hells exercised his power, giving it freely to those who desired it, and entrapping them in the consequences of their greed.

Nadia felt, if but for a moment, a bit of envy for the victims of the lord of the hells. If only she were to be swallowed by him also, her shame and punishment at last coming to an end.

A FEW YEARS LATER, Arioch ascended to the scornful heavens. His crown passed to Benjamin, a younger, kinder king. The guards informed her of the shift in rule but otherwise kept to themselves.

For most of Benjamin's reign, Nadia remained alone beneath the thick kingdom in her dark, cold dungeon cell. She hoped he would remain oblivious to her existence—unaware of the curse his father had left for him to wield. But when he grew older, he discovered her, alone in her ripped black dress, hair tumbling about unclean porcelain skin stretched over her malnourished skeleton.

Tears fell from his eyes when he saw her.

He still made his request.

The honesty curse was no longer enough. The elves had learned silence during interrogations, learned to shape half-truths to avoid consequence. Benjamin spoke of defeats along Arioch's borders and blamed her people for alliances forged in shadow.

All Nadia could feel was relief, hearing her people had survived.

The king appeared only one time at her cell door. In his aged, mangled voice, he ordered her to curse her kind again: the elves would be forced to show their true emotions in the color of their eyes.

The curse sprang from her tongue, commanded by the blood under his control. Arioch had been right—the witch had indeed bound her magic to his loins the moment he spilled her blood.

She hated him for it.

She hated herself more.

Hundreds of years passed, bringing generations of kings and heirs to her cell. They would first grimace at the sight of her, then linger—envy sharpening their eyes as they considered the power they could never possess on their own.

At some point, Nadia started scratching numbers into her cell walls to count the days between kingly visits. It gave her something to do—otherwise, she would try to hibernate the years away. She never made it far before another king interrupted her agony.

Seamas was a king she would never forget. He visited her twice—the first to confirm she was real, the second to beg her to end his life. He claimed she haunted his dreams, denying him peace.

Horrified, Nadia refused. Her magic would not allow such an impure act.

So he let himself into the cell and gutted himself at her feet, his insides spilling over the hard floor where she slept. The guards left his body to rot for a week before sweeping it away.

Nadia didn't sleep a single night while his remains invaded her space.

After that, the visits stopped.

For a year. For a decade.

For five hundred years.

At some point, the guards vanished too. No footsteps echoed down the corridor. No torches flickered beneath her door. She no longer received rations—but to her disappointment, she did not die from hunger. Her skin merely grew translucent over her bones and organs.

She was a corpse with breath in her lungs.

Once, within that stretch of blurred centuries, she gathered her courage and hurled fire at the oak door of her cell. She was surprised when her magic obeyed her, considering her inability to use its pure nature for violence.

She wasn't surprised, however, when her attempt failed horribly.

The oak must have been enchanted, because it did not do so much as blacken.

*You've grown weak.*

Nadia pulled her boney knees into her arms.

She had no need for food or the loving touch of the forest to remain alive. But she wanted company. She desired...touch. Warmth. She wanted to feel something other than cold, see something other than the darkness driving her thoughts to the edges of insanity. She wanted the brush of wind and the scent of elven lavender.

If ever another king came begging for power, she would trade a curse for a single breath of sun. It would be a small request compared to the havoc they demanded of her.

Alone in the silent pitch, with only the occasional wind winding through the dungeon halls, Nadia wondered if her existence had been forgotten altogether.

Five hundred years scraped by with no kings, no guards, no voices.

So when she heard whispers along the dungeon ceiling, she almost believed it was madness.

Loneliness had a way of rotting the mind.

The whispers grew louder.

Nadia hoped desperately she wasn't finally losing her mind. Then, after a few seconds, the whispers were clear enough for Nadia to understand.

"Lords of Arioch, she *is* real," one voice said. It belonged to a young man, and by the tone of his voice, she could tell he was still uncharmed by the cruelties of the world—a perfect target for her escape plan.

"Shh, she can understand our language, you know!" The soldier's boots scuffed sharply against the stone, followed by the metallic *shhhing* of a blade shifting in its sheath.

Nadia scrambled to her feet and peered through the small opening in the door's upper half.

Candlelight revealed the path of two dungeon wanderers. One was dressed in chain mail and the other wore an embroidered tunic and cape. A small crown rested on the tunic wearer's head, and the one in chainmail held a silver pricket—the light from the skinny candle danced across the metal and scattered around Nadia's cell like a glowing diamond in a bouldered cave.

"Yes, I'm very real, young ones." She knew her voice cracked as she spoke, but the elf queen was desperate. *Talk to me. I'm real. I'm alive. I'm here.*

*Let me out.*

The one wearing the circlet must have been close to twenty, and, by his choice of clothing, he had not yet pronounced king. The golden candlelight kindled the adoration in his dark brown eyes, but the soldier to his right seemed nervous. The elf queen gnawed uneasily on her lip.

She tried to suppress her eagerness.

"Your Highness." Nadia spoke as she moved away from the door and got onto her knees to bow. The prince followed her with his eyes, entranced. He blinked and again she crept closer, desperate to confirm this interaction was real. "Tell me, what brings you here?"

"To see if you—"

The soldier elbowed the young prince and Nadia couldn't help but laugh at the silly altercation; it was the first thing that had made her laugh in a long time, aside from her escalating insanity. Hopefully her sudden outburst wouldn't scare the boys away.

The elf queen was often praised for her laugh, many complimenting its musicality. But down here, she worried it was more haunting than beautiful.

"Why are you here? And who are you?" The prince's words changed, his voice struggling to stay even.

The faint redness creeping up the prince's neck confused Nadia momentarily, and then his words dawned on her. *He doesn't know who I am.*

"I could ask the same of you," she said. But she knew who he was. A prince. A Faundor prince. Still, she was cautious. "Who do you *think* I am?"

He wrapped a hand around the iron in the window of the door and peered in at her. "An elf, one trapped here for gods knows how long. Heard the guards whispering about it. We had nothing better to do, so we—"

The young man dressed in chain mail jabbed him again, sealing the prince's lips.

Nadia had already stopped listening. Had her existence truly rotted away? If the princeling didn't know who she was, could Arioch's curse have been forgotten?

Her thoughts darted in all directions.

Had all of this been pointless? The struggle, the curses, the deaths... Her people had suffered for so long, just for all of it to be forgotten? For *her* to live on in eternity, buried beneath the wicked foundations of a human castle?

She would never see the light, not like this. She would need to lie, but she was unpracticed in the art. Could she do it?

She looked into his eyes. He seemed impishly confident, perhaps open to conversation if it served to inflate his ego.

"I'm Nadia," the elf queen introduced herself, "and I'd wager I've been here for far longer than you've been alive, Your Highness."

The shock on the prince's face was irreplicable. "Nonsense! A young lady such as yourself certainly poses no danger to me, nor to Arioch. Tell me, muse, what keeps you here?"

Nadia moved closer to him, her body pressing flush to the door separating them. He staggered back, feet shifting on the dusty ground.

She sensed his desire to turn heel, but she wanted just a hint of a promise that she could count on seeing him again. When she did, she would ask to be released, to see the sun one last time, and return to the forest where she could rest at last.

She worked her mouth, hoping her next lie would come out as easily as the last.

"I am an elf." True. "That is why I've been kept here."

"As I suspected. Then, what crimes have you committed against King Augustus?"

Nadia's eyes widened as she lowered herself beneath the candlelight. The shivering flame made her silky black hair appear as though it were crimson.

*Augustus*. The name was unfamiliar. How long had he been ruling? Had he accomplished anything great?

Nadia stayed quiet. She wasn't ready to answer the prince's trivial question. *Had* she committed any crime? No, at least not against *his* people. Nadia gnawed on her lip, guilt pinching behind her eyes. She'd sinned against her own, and for the past millennium, she was content to pay the price. But who knew of her existence now? Had her people accepted her death? Did they still have hope she would someday return?

Did they even remember the queen who abandoned them?

The elf queen stared blankly at the young men's long shadows cast on the wall behind them. As her mind wandered, the two muttered amongst themselves.

She paid no mind to the conversation, but snapped her head up when she felt the drag of the heavy door against the ground and the clanging of metal as the pricket was placed in her cell.

The candle wobbled in its silver tray, then the flame went steady.

Nadia watched it in fascination. Her thoughts dissolved into wonder.

As she marveled, the door closed and the boys dissolved into the darkness.

Before she realized it, Nadia was alone again.

# I

# INTEREST

When the crown prince was just five years old, he was ordered to drag a blade across his palm. If he flinched, he was unworthy of inheriting the throne.

He did not flinch.

Two decades of duty had followed that first taste of steel. As King Augustus's only son, he now bore the weight of the Faundor bloodline.

New kingdoms had since risen around them, all competing with one another to conquer Arioch, to steal the land back. But each Faundor son was blessed with a divine might that kept these enemies from succeeding. It had been many years since Arioch expanded its territory, and with neighboring kingdoms developing new weapons, agriculture, and customs, it was far more difficult to waltz into enemy territory to claim their land as Arioch had in the history books.

Azriel Faundor knew the books front to back. He knew his enemies, recognized their dirt and sweat-mussed faces on the battlefield. He shed their blood, and he witnessed many of his soldiers die.

Death kept him company, became his friend. He never knew someone as loyal, always there to comfort him. Reliable to a fault.

Apart from the mages that dutifully served the king, the only magical beings allowed within Arioch were the Perri fairies. Viktor was the current heir of the duchy, and he served Azriel with cutthroat severity. The oath his family made many years ago tied them to eternal servitude to the throne. Azriel wouldn't call him a friend, but he provided decent company.

They sat in Azriel's chambers, mulling over their encounter in the dungeon. The fire in the hearth warmed them—the drafty corridors below the castle had given them a particularly unpleasant chill.

The young prince's eyes flicked to Viktor. The white-haired fairy was busy dislodging dirt from under his long fingernails. He wore a bored expression, despite how scared he was to be in the presence of the elven goddess—he had warned Azriel against venturing below to see if she truly existed.

In addition to hearsay, the prince's history books had also hinted at a criminal kings visited once during their reign. Many of the kings' entries were uninteresting to Azriel, but when he stumbled upon the short reign of King Seamas, a diary entry had been inserted between the book's pages. It was a love letter to the elven beauty, recounting her haunting appearance in his dreams, which drove him mad.

Azriel remembered the note and his body stiffened. If his ancestor's infatuation was for the same woman, she'd spoken truthfully about her being much older than he.

Of course, this didn't matter much to him.

After years of death and bloodshed, his heart had, for the first time, bucked to life in his chest at the mere sight of her. He felt immense adoration and curiosity for her even now, in his tower far above where she lived in darkness.

Viktor eyed the dying embers in the hearth, dropped his hands, and moved to add another log to the fire. Azriel stood and fell into his habit of pacing—his footfalls were heavy and his eyebrows knit together.

"I told you," the fairy said, "we shouldn't have ventured down there."

Azriel stilled, sucked in a breath, and glared at his aide. "She's there for a reason, is she not? An elf, kept in the darkest corner of the royal dungeons. Unguarded. Thinner than mist. What kind of crime could she have committed to receive such isolation?"

Viktor seemed to be hiding amusement, the spark in his black eyes the only indicator of mischief. He was well-practiced in controlling his features. Azriel could have ordered Viktor to tell him exactly what he was thinking, but he preferred not to resort to such opaque force, as his father, King Augustus, often did. Instead of verbally answering the prince's rhetorical question, Viktor simply shrugged.

The prince sat in a velvet chair near the fire, resting his chin on a clenched fist. Then, shaking his head, he turned to his confidant and groaned. "You saw how skeletal she was. A frail creature of her likeness couldn't harm me."

Viktor raked a hand through silvery hair before taking a deep breath and blowing it out exasperatedly. His eyes focused on the flames licking hungrily at the fresh wood. "Yes, she could. As you've read, she's lived down there for much longer than we can comprehend. She has power beyond our imaginations. And, if I may remind you, our kinds don't get along with one another. Elves and fairies, that is."

Azriel bristled. He knew Viktor was a fairy, but upon his request, he concealed his tell-tale features so Azriel would routinely forget his true nature. The Perri Duchy was a house full of shapeshifting fairies who groveled before the throne to retain their freedom. Viktor would never be the human companion Azriel wanted, but he didn't care. His father and grandfather couldn't afford to have genuine friendships, and neither could he. Viktor was merely a pawn—a messenger to aid him in battle and a spy who traded in secrets.

Sighing, Azriel leaned into the warmth of his chair. "A cold tea, please."

Viktor clenched his jaw but obeyed, leaving the room to summon a maid.

Azriel stared at his scarred hands hanging between his knees. Years of lashings for improper etiquette had left their mark in the faint, red cracks of healed skin. Back then, Viktor had fed him fairy *elixirs* that mended the wounds quickly, but the memory of King Augustus's scowl lingered in his nightmares. He had learned the hard way what it meant to be the crown prince.

Azriel's thoughts returned to the dungeon, to the porcelain woman with simpering eyes and blacker-than-midnight hair. Her figure was petite, yet regal, and her posture hadn't failed her despite having lived in cramped darkness.

The prince gnawed on his lip as he recalled the woman's calm voice when she addressed him, eyes filled with endless warmth and something else that haunted him.

He'd only ever stared into the cold eyes of his father's court, unfeeling and judging his every move. The court dictated political marriages, so not even he could escape his forthcoming betrothal to Karmin Kittel of Morath, the small kingdom to the west across the Aemorian Sea. Marrying her, he knew, would accelerate his ascension to the throne, and he was to meet her soon. She was five years his junior—just barely a teenager at fourteen. He knew little about her other than her hereditary illness, which would force him to produce an heir earlier in his reign.

He sighed, pushing thoughts of his visit to Morath from his mind.

Why was he thinking of his betrothal? Had his meeting with the elf woman twisted his perspective? He shook his head and relaxed his back into the soft cushions of the chair beneath him.

His body ached from the day's hunt. Before visiting the dungeons, Viktor accompanied Azriel to the forest just outside the castle's training grounds. These woods were sparse, housing few creatures—mostly squirrels and smaller birds—but it was his way of practicing survival between wars. He was accustomed to hunting on foot, though, so riding horseback took a toll on his spine and groin.

He wondered if the elf's body ached, too. *Nadia.* Even the name was beautiful—befitting her ethereal features. Azriel had never seen such a mesmerising creature as she, and he couldn't understand why she'd been jailed.

Or why she hadn't tried to escape.

Viktor re-entered the prince's chambers with a maid. Her expression blank, she curtsied, then hurried around him to his table and placed a tea tray in front of him. She masterfully prepared the tea, adding clear cubes of ice with tongs. They hissed when they drowned in the hot liquid. The maid turned the cup so its floral design faced the prince, then she bowed once more before leaving the room.

Azriel lifted the cup to his lips, sniffed the chilled tea, then sipped. As the herbal drink glaciered down his throat, he leaned forward. "Do you think I could sneak her out of her cell?"

Viktor's thick eyebrows scrunched his forehead. He opened his mouth but nothing came out. Azriel chuckled.

"Just for a little while. I want to hear her story." This earned him another surprised reaction from his aide. Azriel grinned, wide and toothy. "I could use some entertainment, don't you think, Vik?"

The fairy simply sighed, then lifted his own tea to his lips. His was steaming and fresh, the way most people liked it. Azriel preferred drinking the leaves cold—a constant, simmering anger kept his body hot, and cold tea seemed to be the only thing that could calm him.

"I'll take your silence as agreement." Not that Viktor could refuse his final decision, anyway. Members of the duchy were noble by name alone. They served the kingdom more loyally than any servant or soldier, and weren't privy to gossiping about such trivial matters as the prince's nonpolitical interests.

"Your Highness, if I may ask, why must you seek the attention of the elven woman when you've a perfectly capable bride awaiting you in Morath? For all you know, this elf could be—"

Azriel's eyebrows pressed inward at the tone in his friend's voice, and Viktor stopped mid-sentence. "I need not explain the reason for my interest. All will be well as long as I return her to the dungeon when I am finished with her. Don't you agree?"

Viktor studied the prince carefully. "Yes, Your Highness. When would you like to...summon the elf?"

"After our visit to Morath." Azriel smiled, thinking only of Nadia. His thoughts couldn't produce the image of his betrothed when he recently saw the most beautiful woman he'd laid eyes on. His gaze strayed to the fire, and as the flames licked at the hearth, their encounter replayed briefly in his memory—the flickering candlelight warming Nadia's skin, giving color to its ivory smoothness. Her eyes, dark and green and desperate. Hungry.

The prince cradled his teacup in his blemished hands and turned away from the hearth. In a week, he'd be back from his meeting with Karmin. Unless some foreign uproar sought to steal him away, he anticipated seeing Nadia again as soon as he returned. She would no longer wait, curled on the hard ground, eyes frenzied when they'd cracked the door open and offered her their dying candlelight.

Her expression had filled him with a sense of duty and power—he could save her. And then he would have her. She wouldn't be able to refuse him once he opened that door for her... His body heated at the mere prospect, and the tea did nothing to cool it.

Another part of him loathed everything about her condition, wishing to set her free. Though he never spoke of it, he knew that in due time she'd be sacrificed for the king's gain. Every promising, magically proficient elf was taken from the forest and bled over a marble altar; it had been a tradition for generations. What a horrible fate, for such a beautiful thing as Nadia to be bloodied and splayed open, stripped of her magic...

His heart grew sore.

Viktor spoke again, his tone taking on that irritating quality it always did when he was about to advise Azriel against doing what he wished. “If I may, Your Highness—”

Azriel raised a hand. “You may not.”

He squinted at the fire, then at his cup of tea. The cubes of ice clinked against once another, steadily melting into nothing.

Viktor had meant to once again reject Azriel’s missive to bring the elf from her cell. It was a direct betrayal, a breach of trust. The prince’s chest enflamed, and with a steady breath, he tossed his half-full cup of tea into the fire. It shattered at once on the wood and smothered the flames, the hot coals hissing as the cold liquid boiled and evaporated.

Viktor froze, his trembling fingers still looped through his cup’s handle. Liquid sloshed over his pale fingers.

“Well, that’s a pity.” The prince smirked. “It would seem I need a new cup of tea.”

# II
# SALVATION

The candlelight lasted mere moments after the two men left Nadia's cell. Its brevity reminded her of human life—how quickly it appeared and then blipped from the world, leaving her in the endless, inescapable darkness.

She thought of the prince who wasn't yet king. She wondered when he'd be crowned and if she'd ever see him again, or if he would learn of her purpose and demand her to give him the curse *owed* to him.

After a long time, her hand slid against the cold floor and her fingers latched around the thin handle of the silver pricket. The candle was cold—it left an oily residue from the tallow from which it was formed—but it offered her a strange sense of comfort alongside her flickering hope.

It had probably been a week since the princeling visited her. She recalled his deep brown eyes, reflecting the light of the thin candle. It had been a while since she saw someone without a hint of revulsion in their gaze.

She didn't trust it, of course.

She smoothed her thumb over the edge of the metal tray.

He'd been young, too. He could be different from the rest. Maybe he was more light than dark...

A small smile curved into her cheeks as she nestled herself

into a moth-eaten blanket in the corner of her cell, next to stones and other things she'd collected over the years. In the darkness, she'd had plenty of time to become well-acquainted with the space, and she preferred the dark corners where she was most invisible.

Her thoughts briefly held to the hope that the prince would return so she could set her plan in motion to finally leave this place. But those thoughts subsided when she fell into a deep sleep.

Her dreams were loud, replaying memories of her shrieking soldiers, the fairy king's murder, and the human kings who demanded she cast curses upon her own kind. Every death she caused bruised her heart, cut the backs of her knees and sliced across her back, ensuring she knelt before her heavenly mother until the end of time.

She couldn't escape the burden she bore, and the voice of Aldorin rang across all plains of her mind to remind her of her responsibilities as queen of her people. Nadia strained against the words of the goddess. Her chest tightened with a silent scream.

A knife materialized before her, a tempting escape. She hastily grabbed the handle and held it above her chest, her lungs heaving for breath.

She awoke before the blade could give her its mercy.

Three months after the prince visited her, Nadia once again stopped keeping track of time.

Long ago, after someone visited her, she would tally the days until she saw another person again. But...after centuries without seeing a face, she had long ceased the practice.

There also wasn't much room left on the walls; her carved time-keeping marks had begun to overlap one another like ripples in sand.

Though the elf queen stopped scratching lines in the wall—no longer counting the days, weeks, and months—that familiar, biting cold of loneliness consumed her.

With each passing year, her hope dwindled.

She must have spent somewhere between five and ten years in her solitude. Sometimes, she would wonder how long she would have to wait, staring into the darkness. Picturing life beyond her cell. Reimagining her worst nightmares. Hoping the world above was worse than she left it so her isolation would sting less.

Nadia hated herself the moment she had the thought.

She privately vowed to fall onto the first sword she saw. As long as another held the hilt, it wouldn't be considered an act of stealing her own life, which her powers forbade. The elf queen no longer cared about seeing the sun again. She focused on ending her miserable existence as swiftly as possible.

Just when she concluded no one would return for her, the cell door opened. Loud, fast, sudden.

The prince had grown older, and an impressive circlet was woven in to his wispy dark hair. He was alone, without a guard or soldier to accompany him. No one to protect him, she noted. Not that Nadia had planned to do him harm, but at least there wouldn't be anyone standing in her way when she ran the sword at his hip through her stomach.

He just stood there for a moment in the open doorway, velvet capes hanging dreadfully from pins on his shoulders. He hadn't just grown older, but hardened. The naive light Nadia saw in his eyes years ago had left him, but the lines beginning to set in his features were kind. At least, the elf queen desired to see them as such.

Her heart stuttered, and she had to hide her surprise. She clung to the hope that jumped to life inside her.

*I can use him to escape.* It was all she thought.

The prince held a glass encasement of sputtering light. It impressively lit the walls of Nadia's cell, glamouring them with faux sun. For a moment, the elf queen wondered if he'd brought the star with him, that maybe humans could now harness magic.

How impossibly wonderful would *that* be? Then humans would no longer have any reason to keep her there, to oppress her people, to seek dominion over all...

"Nadia." He said her name with a raggedness.

The elf queen swallowed a dry breath, held it in her throat, and waited for the prince to order her to do whatever evil bidding he desired. He would be just like the rest: he'd order her to give him the unobtainable, to do something terrible.

And then he'd be gone.

*No*, her thoughts pressed. She wouldn't let him go until he gave her what *she* wanted in return. He'd trade with her. She'd make it so.

She closed her eyes and a sense of calm settled over her beating heart—something about this endless cycle of human greed was, in a way, comforting. It relaxed her, soothed her before she felt the painful thrum of power which forced her to cast curses on her people. She kept her eyes shut and resigned herself to wait for his command.

But after many long, grueling seconds, no such order came.

Her eyelids reddened as the light neared her. She could feel it —that he would steal her power, then close the door behind him as soon as he got what he wanted. She didn't relax, *wouldn't* relax until—

Something warm and rough clasped her hand, rubbed her pale knuckles with a tenderness she couldn't place. Her thoughts emptied and confusion replaced her resolve. Then, with a tug, she was pulled forward and forward and forward, until she breathed new air and her legs were sweeping in large strides up and up a stone stairwell.

Her heart ached like the fragile tension of a frayed string, ready to break.

The cell door skidded shut, but the sound was distant.

Nadia was terrified, but air steadily filled her lungs again. It tasted different— almost too thick to swallow.

She opened her eyes, but she could barely register the torches and polished stone they passed as they climbed the endless stairs. Had the dungeons always felt so far below? Or was it that she anticipated this moment for so long that it seemed an eternity should pass before they reached the top?

She didn't dare stop the prince from hauling her away, despite how weak her legs were from lack of use, stripped of muscle and made of reedy bones. She followed, finding herself light on her feet as the prince set his brisk pace. His hand steadied her thrice, when she lost her balance or tripped on a step.

Her thoughts whirled. All plans of ending her life had been pulled from under her. Old desires and hopes resurfaced, ones she didn't know still existed. She hadn't needed to convince him to let her out—he did it *himself*.

Would she be free? Would she glimpse the sun?

Possibilities spiraled in her mind.

Would he kill her? Would he make an example of her?

It was freeing to not expect purely good intentions from the prince who once glowed with childlike innocence. Humans had long since proven they were more complex than mere good and evil. They were both. They were neither.

A large oak door revealed itself too quickly, too soon. Her heart thumped in her chest, both frightened and yearning to push through the door and run. Run anywhere. Run nowhere. Run into a sharp stake and end it all before they threw her into a new cell to rot.

The prince reached for the rusted handle. Nadia watched, paralyzed. Her throat tightened into a knot of salt and fear, her knees buckling as the iron began to groan.

The door swung open, but the dark remained absolute. The hope she'd allowed to spark went out with a violent, freezing wrench, leaving her more hollow than the cell itself.

The prince hauled her forward.

The change was a physical blow. Low-burning candelabras lined the stone, their flames fracturing into sickly amber streaks against her unaccustomed eyes. Row after row of iron bars blurred past. Still the dungeons.

The cage had simply grown larger.

A surge of panic stole through her.

Before she realized it, she'd fallen to her knees. The prince stopped walking. He bent over her, the lantern swinging from his hand.

The walls seemed to close in on them, edging toward her crumpled legs, her thin feet. Though glowing candles lit the hall, darkness's claws curled around the light, threatening to smite it.

Nadia knew darkness, and though she feared it, she had to make her home in it.

She now discovered it was more terrifying when there was light for it to take.

Her heart thrummed in her chest, kicking against the walls of her body. She realized with a sudden intensity that she longed to be back in her cell. She wanted to return to the comfort of the cold and damp and hard and dark.

"Nadia," the prince tried again, his voice little more than a rasp. Had Ariochan princes always sounded so underconfident? Or had she hallucinated a royal face onto her captor?

Was he truly the same man who visited her years ago?

She peered up at him, at the orange glow casting light and shadow over chiseled features, brightening the scrape of stubble along his firm jaw. *Ah*, she thought. *There* was that familiar spark in his eye, returned at last. Perhaps the lighting in her cell had tricked her into believing it was gone… or maybe now it was tricking her into believing it had never left.

Her hand lifted, pale and thin and lined with delicate bluish-purple veins. Her fingers curved around the side of his face.

*He's warm,* she thought. The second the words formed in her head, she knew she was foolish to think them. Still, she could not stop her gaze from drifting. To his ears, which were rounded and dotted with freckles. To his stubbled chin. To his bowed lips, which had probably kissed many a maiden.

He stared back at her, his dark eyes sizzling with firelight and something that looked like anger. Nadia turned away, breaking the connection between them.

"Come," was all he said. His hand clasped hers and he led her like a tether through the maze of hallways and stairwells. She didn't misstep again, nor did she focus on the walls that seemed to move from their foundations to follow her.

She let him lead her along. The warm wind brushed her shoulders, and the prince's steady hand grounded her. She closed her eyes, not because she fully trusted him, but because she needed to *feel* this moment. Feel everything.

This was her second mistake.

# III

# CLAIM

Roughly seven years had passed since Azriel last saw her.

War with Midra and the neighboring kingdoms bled from one conflict into the next. In the rare silences of peace, his obsession with her was a fever, a slow-acting madness he couldn't shake.

The instant they returned to the castle, he dismissed his soldiers and ventured deep into the castle's dungeons. Despite his bruised and battered body slowing him down, the reward of seeing her again was a temptation potent enough to carry him all the way.

He hurried to her cell and found her alive. A gift he greedily couldn't wait to open.

She'd followed him without a sound, without a plea. But she also seemed to hesitate, and when she'd fallen behind him and wordlessly expressed her fear with a trembling hand, his heart ached. But then... she'd touched his face. Her silent communication was bold, and he had to take immediate action.

He now pulled her along with a faint grip. Any more, and he feared he might rip her hand from her arm, her arm from her body. The elf's translucent skin was soft and pliable and far too weak.

They were almost to the very top of the chasms of cells. Azriel could smell the spike of rose incense floating in the air.

He longed to view her in the full light of the moon, to see what years of isolation had done to her. He also feared he'd want to send her back for being too impossibly beautiful, too alluring. He already knew he wanted to make *her* his queen instead of Karmin. A wonderful idea, to him and him alone.

He pushed the final oak door into the weapons hall. Moonlight strung in on shadowy bows, slicing the stone walls and floors in diluted color. The elf followed him, then broke free of his hand as she had before. This time, though, she ran beyond him and pressed her small hands to the sill of a wide window.

Her eyes were bright, nearly silver in the night as they mirrored the moon. Her onyx hair was knotted and hung around her in thick ropes, but she was still beautiful. *So breathtakingly beautiful.* The dirty rags covering her chest and legs seemed weightless on her, as though a gust of wind might tear them from her wiry frame. Thin porcelain legs shot from the dark cloth, her arms the trails of falling stars. *Mesmerising.*

She took an audible breath, and Azriel realized she was probably smelling fresh air for the first time in many years. A feeling like guilt wrenched in his chest. Alongside it, his desire for her smoldered.

"Nadia." He had already started a few times already, but that's where his tongue stopped him. Nothing would come after that. What could he say? They were strangers, and he'd gone to her late in the night. What reason did he have for bringing her here?

He knew. Why was he loath to admit it?

She turned and looked at him. Though the moon was the only light in the hall, she seemed to glow as a separate entity. She was frail and weak and powerless here, but she was also everything else—beautiful, strong, free, his. *His.*

"Tell me your name." Her voice was raw from lack of use.

He tried to hide the excitement that tore its way to the surface and threatened to spread across his lips. With a step toward her, he said, "Azriel Faundor, Crown Prince of Arioch and First Captain of King Augustus's Legion of Knights."

For a moment, she seemed to merely stare at him, to study him. In that moment, he felt a strong thrum of power from her, something ancient. The second he felt it, it was gone. And it was like it had meant to be there, nestled next to him. A power that *belonged* to him. He gulped.

Her gaze snagged on his and something like understanding flickered across her features. He couldn't tell what thoughts whirred behind her sparkling eyes, but he was surprised to find life there, especially after she'd been so far away from everything for so long.

"Your Highness." She trembled as she dipped her head.

Azriel delighted in her politeness. "And you are Nadia."

She nodded once, then turned to face the moon, which hung in the sky like a pristine silver disc. But the moon was incomparable.

"I want to know you. Your past. Anything you're willing to profess." The words tumbled out of him. His hands were growing clammy, itchy. He wanted to *touch* her. He sucked in a breath and his fingernails bit into his calloused palms.

She was still for a moment, her body stiffening. Then, a shiver shook her shoulders and her lips quivered. Her mouth moved slightly, but no sound came out.

Azriel cocked his head to the side, but she didn't respond to his curiosity. With a sudden urge to hear her speak again, he closed the distance between them. Just inches away, he could make out the soft whisper of her words. Her eyes moistened as she spoke.

"Please let me out. I'll do anything you want. I want nothing more than to see the sky once more, the sun beating on my skin. I want to taste food, to vomit when I've had too much. I want to see the forest. Please let me out. I'll do anything you want. I want nothing more than to—"

He recoiled as she rambled on, her tongue twisting as though under a spell. Her face was blank as she recited her pleas, and she didn't react even when Azriel stepped around her.

"—to taste food, and vomit when I've had too much. I—"

He slid his hand under her jaw and made her face him. She was soft, warm, delicate.

She tensed. The words halted on her thin lips.

He smiled at her. She blinked at him, desperation swimming in her eyes. He knew that look well, because he'd seen it a countless number of times on the battlefield. Determination. Grit.

She wanted to survive.

He didn't know how long she'd been trapped in the depths, just that it was long enough that she didn't *want* food, light, the sun; she *needed them*. She also needed *him*, he realized. Just like he needed her. Hungered for her.

His grin grew wider as an invisible heat flooded his ears.

He tilted her chin and moved his body so his hips pressed lightly against her, the small of her back resting against the windowsill.

Her eyes fluttered shut and her body shuddered, but he held her steady. He slid his hands up her soft, thin arms, then wrapped one arm around her waist.

He was new to this. This kind of longing. He hadn't known he could feel such burning, deep desire. He didn't think he deserved it, didn't think he'd be able to control himself once he had a taste of her.

She rested her hand under his jaw and stared with glossy eyes at his lips. Her finger drifted to them, her feather-light touch sending a shiver down his spine.

She was just as touch-starved as he.

*Thank the gods.*

One of his hands cradled her jaw, and he bent to kiss her.

She gasped against his mouth, but her surprise was smothered by the harder press of his lips. Her hands twitched, then nestled against the back of his neck as she kissed him back, her lips unpracticed yet desperate.

That new hunger continued growing in him, but he knew this was not the place for it. He needed to control himself. At least, until they had more privacy.

He was the first to pull from her. Her gaze was hazy, her lips swollen. Her body swayed as though influenced by drink. He grasped her hand firmly, tugged her from the weapons hall, and brought her to his bedchamber. His belongings hadn't yet been moved to the king's quarters, which he once complained about but was now thankful for. Karmin's belongings had already been delivered to the king's chamber, and he didn't want the reminder of his forthcoming wedding to ruin the moment he'd longed seven years for.

When Azriel lifted Nadia, he was shocked at how light she was. The surprise was easily smudged away when she blinked at him with feverish eyes.

He laid her upon his bedcovers, and as she removed her clothing, he was dumbstruck, unable to move. The scraps she wore she tossed aside without much care. Her hair fanned around her. Azriel drew in a labored breath.

He hadn't seen a woman naked in some time, and he'd never viewed an elven woman like *this* before—pristine, like carved marble. He was more accustomed to seeing their bare bodies broken and presented on an altar for Arioch, but hers was perfectly formed, her curves begging to be touched and coddled. Breathing, alive, warm.

He didn't think himself to be much of a redeeming character, but he still forced himself to ask, "Are you sure? We can wait."

*He* could not. But if she changed her mind, he supposed he would oblige her.

She responded with a smile. It tilted one way, and her white skin dimpled at the mouth.

It completely shattered his resolve.

Desire burned through him, and he gave into its greedy, controlling hands.

Azriel unpinned his robes and removed the tunic at his waist. Soon, he was also bare before her. Her expression showed hints of exhaustion and delirium, but she still seemed fully aware of what they were about to do. He was not evil. He would not force himself upon her if she did not allow it.

He swayed above her, smiling like a boy. He no longer hid the satisfaction of finally *having* her. He'd waited so long, he'd been so *patient*. Now he would receive his reward.

His lips crushed against hers.

He had much on his mind, including matters of his impending coronation he needed to take care of, but despite all of this, he decided for one night he'd forget it all. It was easy, too. With her, it was *so easy*.

It may have been a sort of devious magic Nadia cast upon him, or maybe it was magic of a purer intent, sent from his ancestor Arioch, himself. But as they filled the night with each other's company, fitting their bodies snugly against each other, Azriel knew she was the one he'd been waiting for.

He would never let her go.

# IV

# SICKNESS

Political alliances were far more important than trivial matters such as love—this was why kings took concubines. Azriel had never felt strongly enough about any of the women he bedded to desire any of them as permanent bedmates, but now he understood why his predecessors were adamant about keeping the harem tradition alive.

Nadia was the spark to a flame, and in the seven years since he last saw her, the flame grew into a wicked fire. She was an elf, true, and he, a Faundor royal. This made it impossible to make her his queen, even though that was what he desired.

Azriel woke before Nadia, and she continued to sleep soundlessly while he admired her. He ran a hand along her cheek, then allowed it to travel to her neck, her waist, her hip... He feared he would lose his passion for her, as he had before with every other courting, but he found his attraction to her was stronger than ever, especially after having shared his bed.

He wished to ravish her, to make her ache for him in the way he ached for her.

He groaned when a servant's knock came at the door, reminding him of his responsibilities—the meetings he had to attend were unfortunately not the kind he could escape. So he carefully drew the covers away and slipped into a fresh tunic, then pinned a new robe to his shoulders. He placed his circlet atop his head of mussed dark brown hair, and then, without a word, he left the room and started down the corridor to the war strategy discussion chamber.

A long table filled the length of the room. Nobles were already seated and discussing uninteresting topics with one another. Steaming plates of duck, potatoes, venison, and marbled lamb were placed in front of each of them, untouched until the king gave the order.

Viktor sat with his fingers steepled together, a mask of indifference stiffening his features. His father, the previous duke, died while they were defending the border to the northeast, so Viktor was adjusting to his new position. Between their time away from the castle and his recent inheritance, Azriel knew the young fairy was more overwhelmed than he appeared.

When Azriel sat next to Viktor, King Augustus raised a hand to silence the room.

He was considered a wise king, but Azriel knew this was merely due to his age. Other kingdoms might see an aging ruler as an opportunity to seize power, but the Faundor line had always maintained an unbroken and orderly succession. It made things simpler when each queen only bore one child, and it was always (praise be to Arioch) a son. Those born of lesser unions were half-siblings and thus were treated accordingly. Most bastard children were married off to other kingdoms, quietly accepting the humility that came with their illegitimacy. Azriel had only one sibling, a half-sister, born four years after him by accident rather than design. When she turned fifteen, Augustus sent her to Midra to marry a minister, who was well beneath her station but was expected to treat her well enough.

As the legitimate son, Azriel was favored by fate, yet with the crown still beyond his grasp and his father soon to retire to a quiet estate in the country, a growing restlessness troubled him. Azriel was raised his entire life knowing this position belonged to him, and yet, seeing his father age and leave the throne to him made him realize just how impermanent the title of king truly was.

Once Azriel became king, he would no longer be able to leave the castle for lengthy periods. He wouldn't be fighting on the front lines to protect the kingdom from invasions or threats.

"I will abdicate in two weeks' time, before the Feast of Undying. My son, Azriel, will soon be your new king." Augustus's voice was solid, final. There was no room for doubt or denial. Denial was treasonous.

Silence hovered over the table, but not for long.

Viktor cleared his throat, and all attention turned to him.

"If I may speak freely, Your Majesty." The white-haired duke stood, and Azriel's chest tightened. The air grew taut. Viktor smiled faintly. "With His Highness's coronation and marriage growing near, we must ensure our kingdom's defenses are not left unattended. Our kingdom will weaken without a warrior to lead our charges."

Augustus regarded the duke with a slow, feline blink, his fingers tracing thoughtfully along his beard. A dry smile curved his lips before he released a low chuckle. "Indeed, Duke Perri. A new captain shall be appointed soon. Tell me. Have you someone in mind?"

Viktor bowed. "Yes, Your Majesty. My wife is with child, and from the strength of her pulse and her worsening symptoms, we believe she carries a son. As you know, the men of our line are fierce from birth and require constant tending. I offer myself and my charge in service, in return for aid to be granted my wife in her confinement."

Augustus raised a brow. "Your blood binds you to our service. Favors are not the reward of obedience. Your father knew his place well enough. Do you now presume your charge exceeds that of my son?"

Viktor looked at the prince then. Something like helplessness conflicted over his features.

Azriel blinked away, his chest remaining tight. It had been a few years since he spoke with his aide-turned-duke, their last conversation occurring during the previous duke's memorial. They were little more than now, yet the look Viktor gave him carried a trace of misplaced faith. Azriel wouldn't stand by him, not after the fairy confessed to Augustus their trespass in the dungeons, and his intent to free her seven years ago.

This, Azriel wasn't certain of. He'd merely made a conjecture when wars stacked upon each other with little room to rest between. He could only come to one conclusion: that his father knew of his discovery, and wished to send him away for as long as possible.

Azriel flexed his hand into a fist.

"Not in physical strength, but in our ability to use magic, Your Majesty. Our family possesses a special ability to create elixirs from enchanted woodland herbs and roots. They will be of great help to your son, and can also be used against adversaries in battle." As Viktor spoke, the entire room listened intently. Some gasped. This new information was spoken so simply, as though Viktor assumed it was common knowledge.

Augustus coughed. A fist went to his mouth as he continued to gargle, and when he pulled it away, his fingers came away bloody.

The table of nobles was silent again.

"Such important power..." Augustus's voice was rough when he spoke again. "How long have you kept this from me? From my entire lineage?" The rage was clear in his voice, the intimidation bearing a similar quality to the magic Azriel often felt when he encountered it on the battlefield.

Viktor raised his hands in defense. His eyes widened and panic siphoned the color from his already-pale face. "Allow me to apologize, Your Majesty. I have offended you." He slid from his seat and dropped to one knee, his head just barely visible above the table. "You may punish me as you see appropriate. I was unaware my forefathers hadn't revealed this knowledge to you. I only recently found out about it, myself, when I inherited my father's seat. However, my offer stands. These elixirs are to be used for the benefit of your bloodline. You have my word."

The king huffed, his body relaxing. "Very well. You are excused. Deliver your plan to me by dawn tomorrow. You know what awaits, should you come unprepared."

Viktor nodded, crossing an arm over his chest in salute.

"Is there anyone else who wishes to defy me? Or shall we proceed with the subject of Azriel's court?"

No one breathed a word.

Azriel silently cursed Viktor for his cunning—for using his wife and child to secure Augustus's favor. He had long suspected his aide hungered for power, but he knew the oath binding Viktor's blood to the throne left him little room to act. Azriel's forthcoming ascension provided the opening the fairy duke had waited for.

"My son," Augustus said. "Lady Karmin awaits you in your chambers. You are to consummate the marriage before your coronation. Beget a son who will strengthen the long line of Faundor blood. I expect word of her condition before I depart for The Valley."

Azriel's fists tightened, his eyes angling in a glare at the duke who reclaimed his seat next to him. Though Viktor met his stare with practiced indifference, Azriel knew it was no coincidence. The fairy's defiance was plain enough.

"I've met Lady Karmin only once." Azriel watched Viktor, who picked absently at his leather gloves. "I'm not so sure she will be easily persuaded to my bed as you think."

Azriel's memory of Karmin was colorless in comparison to his experience with Nadia. He allowed that Karmin was the perfect picture of a marriageable noblewoman, but she clearly had no interest in Azriel. When they first met—her, thirteen, and Azriel, eighteen—she'd been far more taken with her embroidery than with the notion of marriage. They hadn't met since, but in the seven years that passed, she ought to have matured in many ways. Azriel doubted she'd developed any real interest in him in their time apart, yet he admitted to being mildly curious about what opinion she held of him now. She would be queen, after all—and surely that meant something to her.

Morath had no princess of its own, but Karmin's closeness to the royal family made her the nearest thing to it. King Ordyr deemed her a suitable match—one who could unite the kingdoms well enough. Both he and King Augustus regarded the union as a prudent political alliance.

Karmin awaited him in the king's royal bedchambers, while a slumbering elf lay in his princely bed.

He wondered momentarily if an elf could bear the child of a human lover...

"Then force her," Augustus said, as though the answer was a given.

Azriel froze.

The king flexed his fingers. "She is frail. It's a wonder she's lived to see twenty. Childbearing will take its toll. You must not delay. She knows this just as well."

This was not about forcing Karmin to bear his child—the hardened scowl on Augustus's pale face demanded *obedience.* This was an *order*, and Azriel, still a prince, was compelled to obey.

"I will take other women to bed," Azriel sputtered. "Such things have been done before, have they not? It would be no great feat to claim one of their sons as the queen's before she dies."

Augustus pounded a fist on the table. Flinches rippled across the noblemen.

"Mockery!" Augustus boomed. "How dare you defile the purity of our bloodline! Azriel, you are a man of five-and-twenty, and you shall provide me a grandson. He will succeed you. No more of this insolence. An illegitimate child can never claim the Faundor name. To permit such a thing would shatter the line of power we have forged since the founding of our kingdom."

Azriel fumed, but stayed quiet, flexing his fingers in and out of fists to steady himself. Viktor shifted slightly, but Azriel did not glance at him.

"You shall soon learn what it means to keep our line pure. It is a secret not even I knew before ascending the throne. It is a secret you must take to your death, even if threatened at swordpoint. Even if the kingdom has crumbled under your feet."

Azriel inclined his head. The kingdom held countless secrets, and all weighed heavily upon the one who wore the crown. Yet he could not think he would comprehend them, even if every one were revealed. Such was the nature of the secrets entrusted to Faundor kings.

To speak aloud the secrets soon to pass between them, before the assembled nobility, testified to the power Augustus wielded—and the power Azriel would soon inherit.

"I understand, Your Majesty," Azriel conceded. His father grunted.

"Four days after your coronation, your wedding will be held. At that same hour, Lady Karmin's pregnancy shall be made known to the court."

Azriel knew not to argue. He simply nodded. "Yes, Your Majesty."

Once king, he would no longer bow and beg and kiss the feet of his wrinkled father. He would have his wife, and if she died from her illness before birthing their child, he would have no choice but to select her replacement. He understood the necessity of an heir, and could not afford for his new court to see him as weak or foolish.

"Viktor will no longer serve beside you. He shall act for the kingdom and command its wars in your name." The king's hand swept shakily across the table. "These men and their sons are to sit upon your council. Of their daughters, select as many as you please to attend your court, and from them may be chosen your concubines." No one at the table dared voice disagreement. "If there are others you wish to admit to your council, it may be done only once you have ascended. Until then, I will permit no interference."

Azriel's jaw tensed. The air in the room cooled immediately, the meals still untouched—mere pleasantry. Confrontations of this degree often ended in blood, so he was surprised when his father raised but a single hand.

"Dismissed."

"You retrieved her." Viktor seethed as he followed Azriel out of the meeting room.

The prince met the fairy's glare with a smirk. "It's lovely to see you too, old friend." Azriel crossed his arms over his chest. "Do you truly question my authority? I hold your fortunes in my hand, and it's been long since you served at my side. I alone decide who I lift from the dungeons, *and* whether or not I take her to my bed."

Viktor cursed under his breath and turned on his heel, making for the servants' quarters.

"Remain where you are." The moment Azriel growled the order, he felt the tether of power leashing the fairy to him.

Viktor's feet stayed rooted, and a startled noise escaped him. "Surely you didn't break our years of silence to *scold* me, Viktor?"

"I would not dare," Viktor said. Azriel's fist itched to strike at the mere tone of the duke's voice, but he held himself, a rare calm keeping his fury at bay.

"It is pleasing to see even you cannot defy me when I issue a command." Azriel clicked his tongue, smiling as the color drained from the duke's face. "Come, then. Follow me to my chambers. We shall resume this discussion in the library."

Viktor's jaw ticked, his eyebrows steep silver slashes over dark eyes. His body stiffly turned, keeping his distance as Azriel led the way to the king's private chambers.

Inside the room, tall archtop windows glided along the east wall, and the sunlight brought a warm glow to the main room. The hearth on the west wall was cloaked in shadow, and the settee and stools facing it were vacant. Azriel surveyed the room with disinterest, but his eye caught on the figure sitting atop the enormous four poster bed, which was the only item he hadn't replaced in the large room. He squinted past the glare of sun and met the curious gaze of a young woman. Her hair was dark, but he couldn't determine the color in the muted dark. Something between black blood and dark night.

She snapped a book shut and stood to greet him. When the hem of her skirt met the light, Azriel raised a hand.

Why did he halt her? Could it be he feared her maturity? Or was it that she had grown into a woman worthy of queenship?

A feeling of disgust curdled in his stomach.

"Follow one of my manservants to the gardens. I shall see you at dinner." His voice left no room for reply as he turned and guided Viktor to the hearth.

"Your Highness, I—"

Her voice had grown deeper, shedding its chirp for the

mournful cadence of a lament. Azriel's body froze at the desperation it carried, and then his blood burned with fury.

"You may leave now." The prince didn't turn to look as his betrothed drew her skirts with a sharp exhale and left the bedchamber.

Viktor turned to him, his face drawn in severe lines. A duke by title, yet Azriel relished commanding him as though he were a man of lesser station. The fairy's expression flickered with restraint, but Azriel knew it would crumble under steady pressure.

"Light the hearth," Azriel purred. He watched as the duke moved mechanically to pull freshly cut logs from a stack next to the fireplace. As he tossed them in, Azriel continued their earlier conversation. "You vanished for a time, and there is much to speak of. Our long years away from the castle weigh upon us. Though wars are inevitable, their swift succession makes me wonder at your hand in them. Speak of your dealings with my father, the king."

The fire sparked to life, and Viktor fanned it lightly until the flames grew and licked around the pale wood. It crackled and popped in the hearth, and for a moment that was their only accompaniment as Azriel studied Viktor through a squint.

Viktor's throat bobbed as he returned to the prince's side. His lips parted, then popped shut. His eyebrows slanted downward.

"You suspect I created opportunities to...keep you away from your mistress, Your Highness?"

Azriel's lips pulled away from his teeth, rising into a grin that quickly turned sour. "How could she have been my mistress when I had met her but once, and she languished in a cell while we were away?"

Viktor breathed deeply, but said nothing. His hands stiffened and clenched until his nails bit into the meat of his leather-covered palms.

Azriel clicked his tongue in satisfaction. "After one war was won, you dragged me into another, and another, and another until your father's illness forced your return. Answer me now, before I lose my temper: You knew of the elf before I did, and sought to keep me from her. Seeing my interest, you took it upon yourself to separate us for as long as you could."

Viktor swallowed. The prince was being entirely unfair—the Perri family was dutifully bound to the throne, with no choice but to serve whoever sat upon it until death, as long as its occupant was from the Faundor family. Any protest would be meaningless, so he remained silent, eyes fixed on the floor.

Azriel's fist struck the settee. "Answer me, damn you!"

Viktor flinched, then nodded. He had known of the elf long before Azriel's fateful discovery. For centuries, the Perri duchy had kept her existence hidden from every human ruler—a living secret, older than many kingdoms, and dangerous to any who crossed her path. Even as duke, Viktor had barely begun to understand the depth of his people's history.

The fire crackled in the hearth, and Viktor's jaw ticked as he watched the flames. Soon he would serve King Azriel, and he would need to tread carefully. The knowledge he possessed could not remain hidden forever, and now, the prince was deliberately drawing it out.

"She's a threat, Your Highness."

"Surely not," Azriel snapped. "You've seen her. She's mere skin and bones and pale blue veins." The prince chuckled darkly as he lifted a hand to fix the alignment of a thick gold ring on his index finger. "Her weakness becomes her, wouldn't you agree?"

Viktor flexed his hands. His eyes flicked to the door, indicating his sudden desire to flee. Azriel studied him, amused at his discomfort.

"As she is now, she can do you no harm, Your Highness."

Viktor sounded defeated. Whether for Azriel's benefit or not, the prince took the cue.

"Bring me elixirs to conceal her magic and her appearance... the same your Perri family uses to disguise their true forms. I will see to it you have no reason to question her presence in my castle."

He dismissed the duke with a wave of his hand. Viktor bowed and turned from the room, forcing measured breaths to calm his stiff arms. Azriel narrowed his glare at the duke until his coattails disappeared down the hall.

AFTER HE WAS sure Viktor was far enough away, Azriel slinked from the king's bedchamber and returned to his princely rooms.

He released a breath when he found Nadia nestled in the large blankets that crumpled around her, still asleep.

The maids informed him they'd bathed and dressed her before she crawled back into the tall bed, and so he had no reason to worry.

When he pulled the covers away to look at her, his breath hitched and heart sang.

She wore a thin gown of pearly silk, so much like her own skin, he had to blink several times to convince himself she wore any clothing at all. Her knees tucked into her chest like a small child's. Her long, black hair spun around her like the ever-moving night sky, draping over her sparkling gown in webs of dark. It was already high-noon, and the light filtering through the tall windows bathed her in an ethereal glow that pronounced her unreal beauty.

He knelt before her, dismissing the maids from the room as he did. And then he just...watched her. Allowed his body to remember the *feel* of her. He didn't dare disturb her when she appeared so peaceful, her chest rising and falling evenly. He wondered when she had last slept so soundly—it was certainly the first time she'd slept in a bed in years.

Her slow, steady breaths bowed her sides and the outline of her ribs bent through the thin fabric. The sight made his stomach turn.

He wondered, briefly, if he had harmed her. Both shared a passion—for him, it rang true in his soul, but for her, it likely resulted from years of loneliness. He could be the answer to whatever dreams played across her memory, whatever desires controlled her delicate fingers...

He was anxious to learn more about her, to love her in a way he'd wanted to love a woman for so long.

But not now. Now, he felt the best he could do for her was to allow her time to rest and recover.

He stood and left the room. Maids awaited him, bowing when he walked past.

"See to it she's fed as soon as she wakes," he ordered. "And let her want for nothing. Give her anything she asks for." Then, with a confident step down the corridor, he smiled to himself.

# V

# DEBT

Nadia cradled the warm black mug, the heat creeping into her fingers and traveling up her arms to the center of her drained soul.

The brownish liquid smelled of roses and earth, and it tasted quite bitter, but she hadn't drank or eaten in years, and her body had long-missed the satisfaction of quenching her thirst. In several long gulps, she emptied her mug. Her heart warmed and her skin prickled with pleasure. She felt her muscles yawn from their thousand-year hibernation.

The night before lingered in fragments, each one a reminder of the sin she had shared with the heir of Arioch. She felt the echo of his touch, and nausea churned in her gut, threatening to spill. *What had she* done?

She stared blankly at her empty cup, and one of the maids tending to her bowed before plucking it gingerly from Nadia's fingers.

The maids had stopped in to assist her into nicer clothes and offered her food and drink, but they were quiet, cautious, and clearly wary of the elven queen. Nadia had hoped their silence might signal welcome, but when her questions went unanswered, she saw it for what it was: a bidden silence, not voluntary.

She could not discern whether her people were hated, forgotten, enslaved, or something else entirely. Though her long ears and undying body marked her as one of the goddess's own, the maids' faces betrayed no malice. In fact, they did their best to avoid looking at her directly.

The maids took their leave once they confirmed Nadia wanted for nothing else. The elf queen was glad for the silence at first, but once she was alone, her pulse thudded in her veins. She scanned the room, seeing the tall windows for the first time, the *sun* shining through them.

Confusion washed over her.

Why had the princeling released her? Why had he given her a bed to sleep in and maids to attend to her? Why had he bedded her without first hearing who she was and why she was locked in the dungeons?

*For power.* Nadia's thoughts nearly shrieked at her. *Why else had any of the* other *Faundor kings taken an interest in you?*

Nadia's breath caught in her throat once more, and this time she couldn't pull another breath in. She choked.

*A new prison,* her thoughts continued in her mind. *You may have escaped the darkness, but you won't ever be able to leave, not when a* human *prince stole your purity and now claims you as his own.*

The light from the sun dimmed slightly, and Nadia scrambled to her feet, entirely malleable to the distraction. She was sore from walking up many flights of stairs and spending the night with the prince, but she was determined to reach the large window—she *had* to see the sun before it disappeared, or she would never get a chance to see it again.

Her room was high up, overlooking crowned towers and gates colored with white marble and gold. Gardens filled the area below, flush with reddening maple trees and bushes of winking red berries. A fountain bloomed at both corners, each carved into the shape of an animal from the Aldorin forest—dragons, fish, and birds were fashioned from marble. Sequestered among breezy white flowers, a woman in an elaborate dark blue dress sat against a tree, like a blot of ink on a painted canvas. She held a book in front of her face.

Nadia turned her chin to the sky. The cloud concealing the golden sun blew away, and the rays shone brilliantly. Her heart jumped to life. The warmth, the natural light—everything she thought she would never see again–was here before her once more. The gods had answered her pleas. Her heart could fail her now, and she would die happy.

"Good morning," a voice chuckled behind her. "Or should I say afternoon... evening? You slept most of the day."

Nadia started. Her senses were still adjusting to the bright world above her dungeon cell, and she'd not realized someone had joined her in the room. But as Prince Azriel's was the only male voice she'd heard for years, she recognized it instantly.

A faint blush crept across her cheeks as she braced herself on the window sill. She lingered a moment, gathering courage, before turning to him with a small, hesitant smile.

Memories from last night chased her. Brief, hot, mortifying.

She pushed them aside, ashamed that her tired, desperate mind believed *that* was what love was. A moment of vulnerability twisted hand in hand with lust, perverted under the guise of her freedom.

He stepped beside her, and it might have been her imagination, but he seemed to put a purposeful amount of distance between them. His hands rested on the ledge of the large window, fingers dressed with sparkling gold and amethyst rings. In the light, she saw he wasn't all that terrible-looking, for a human.

Shame washed over her the moment she had the thought. But she sought to rationalize it, anyway.

He'd grown into a fine young man, with a beard stippling his jaw and chiseled to shape his square face. He had royal cheekbones, not unlike her own, but his face was much meatier. His eyes were dark, almost black, like his hair. Though Nadia was tall for an elf, he was at least two heads taller. She noted the crown on his head was not the ancient one passed down from king to king, and his clothing was simple, yet elegant: brown leather shoes, a white tunic with golden needlework, and black trousers. From this much, she could tell he was not yet king, but Nadia wondered if that day was quickly approaching. Arioch's kings didn't seem to live longer than half a century—Nadia couldn't recall a single instance where she met a white-haired royal.

"I hope you find this room to be agreeable." He tilted his head to meet her gaze.

Heat rushed to Nadia's cheeks as she snapped her attention to the sparkling kingdom below. The woman in the blue dress had disappeared.

As silence conquered the space between them, for a moment Nadia felt like she could breathe, adjusting herself to the prince's presence at last. He had given her distance immediately—perhaps he, too, was ashamed of their rushed night together...

Azriel's large hand brushed over hers. She tried to hide her surprise, but when she looked into his eyes, she noticed a familiar blend of emotions that corrupted them: worry, fear, desperation.

Though she tried to suppress them, memories of the previous night covered her arms in gooseflesh and whipped her frantic heart into a frenzy. She clenched her fist beneath his hand.

What a terrible mistake she'd made!

"I worry for you, Nadia. I must confess, I'm rather ashamed of my actions. You're—" He lifted his hand to her cheek and brushed his knuckles down to her chin. His jaw tightened. "—terribly thin. Do elves not die of starvation?" He glanced at their hands, now intertwined together, then locked her in place with his gaze. His voice came out in a low rumble. "You're colder than ice, Nadia. I'm certain I ordered the maids to bring you tea..." His words brimmed with anger. Thick eyebrows knotted over cold irises.

The expression was all too familiar to the elf queen.

With a shaky breath, Nadia slipped away from the prince and tucked a strand of silvery black hair behind her ear. She didn't look at him as she said, "Yes, they brought me tea. Thank you."

Azriel nodded. Then, thoughtfully, he turned to the window. "Tell me, did they feed you... down there?" His words were ruffled, uncertain.

Nadia considered him, disbelief twisting in her gut. How could he not have known? He had come for her, yet surely he must have noticed her hollow cheeks, the gauntness beneath her eyes, the sharp weight of her bones. Or had her magic preserved her outward form so well that even he could not tell? She had yet to see her reflection, but she felt... empty, and imagined she must look it as well.

"No, they did not." Her voice was icy, despite the effort she made to keep it level. Her body was confused, desiring to share his warmth after their intimate night, and simultaneously wishing to run far, far away.

She gnawed on her lip to distract herself from her indecision.

A muscle ticked in his jaw, and his eyes sparkled with a darkness that sent a shiver down Nadia's spine. He looked as though he wanted to kill someone... or some*thing*.

"Damn them for the way they treated you."

Nadia blinked at him. She didn't know how to respond—shocked, flattered, frightened? His voice sounded fractured, distraught. But she simply did what she knew to do best: she masked her reaction with as blank an expression as she could manage. Since when did a human ever pity her like this, grown *upset* with the other humans who caused her so much suffering?

Her thoughts screamed at her.

*Trap. This is a trap.*

The prince continued, "Since the day I met you in the dungeon, you've occupied my dreams, my strategy meetings, my conversations. In the most inopportune moments, I could only think of you, even as I became helplessly betrothed to another. That day, seven years past, I was but a boy, yet I'd already been captivated by you. And though I may never see you as my queen, I..."

He shook his head, unable to continue, and he turned away from the window. His jaw tensed as he walked along the length of the room, stopping to face the large gilded wall. Hands ran through wiry black hair, then scratched the beard starting along his jaw.

He sounded genuinely conflicted... He was beginning to sound more and more like Seamas, the king who'd commanded her to take his life as punishment for his obsession with her. Her mind spiraled at what horrors she might witness if she were to refuse *this* prince, too. Would he ask the same of her... or worse?

"Love," Nadia croaked. Azriel jerked his head up. "It is a very serious thing. Elves may bond but once, and that bond endures until death. Humans know no such permanence, marrying instead for fragile peace, easily broken should they separate."

And how Nadia envied the women she counseled many years ago, their worries bundled in an easy-to-understand combination of romance and expectation. Many of them found their fated lovers, and all of them became incredibly happy, bearing many children.

A queen was not allowed to want. She was meant to be a symbol—spotless, sanctified. Untouched.

And she *had* been. Until last night.

Guilt crept along the back of her neck. Or perhaps it was Aldorin's breath, whispering of her sins against the goddess. *You have foresaken your purity.*

The prince stalked over to her, a heaviness to his steps as he closed the distance.

"Indeed, we have something far more fleeting." His hand rose slowly, seeking permission to touch her. When she did not move, he took it as consent, cupping her soft cheek. She froze beneath his touch, but he did not notice. "Yet therein lies its beauty. We are not bound by magic. Instead, we *choose* to remain with our lovers, each day, by our own will."

*Or to leave,* Nadia thought. Oh how she wished to leave.

The prince's warm hand traveled down her neck. His thumb brushed along her smooth jaw and his eyes wandered, first to her cheek, then to her neck, to the length of her body, and finally returned to settle on her lips.

With little effort, the prince pulled her closer to him, angled his head downward, and brought his mouth just a breath away from hers. Nadia's eyes squeezed shut and her heart hammered in her chest, drumming to a familiar rhythm. She hadn't been herself last night, hungry for company and finally *warm. It had not been worth it.* The rhythm of her heart sent tremors along her arms. It was not *love*, she realized with a finality.

It was fear.

She was terrified her mistake had made her his property. That, because he now *owned her*, he would never let her go.

His pine and lavender breath was all she could smell, taste, feel. He didn't move any closer, and their lips never made contact, but their intimate proximity rattled her with a dread she hadn't possessed since she lost King Elias on the battlefield. Memories invaded her mind—of Elias's body being lifted above the carnage, skewered by the talons of Arioch's dragon, the life absent from his widened eyes.

She deserved much worse for what she had done. The thousand years in her cell could never pay for the atrocity she committed with the crown prince. It was a new sin, one that would forever taint her.

She knew when Azriel leaned away, for his scent lingered, but there was no longer any heat. When she opened her eyes, he was staring at her from a comfortable distance, his expression indecipherable. She held her breath, her hands pressed to the windowsill. The sun was beginning to burn her arm, but she didn't mind. She welcomed the painful distraction.

"You're mated to another." His words were cold, accusatory. "It is why you refuse me, why you tremble before me."

Nadia choked on the breath she'd been holding. She avoided his gaze, sifting through her memories. The goddess Aldorin blessed mated pairs with a ritual mark, a sign of their bond. She bore no such mark, but how likely was it that Azriel would know this about her people? She gnawed on her lip.

She didn't know the prince, she couldn't read him. And yet, she felt a strange desire to explain herself, to explain *everything* to him. He was the first person she'd been so intimate with, so... *close.*

Maybe she was in a mere state of frenzied confusion. Maybe he truly planned on discarding her once he got his use out of her. Or maybe, for the first time in forever, her heart was right—maybe it would be alright if she gave herself permission to *hope,* one last time.

"No," she said. The prince arched an eyebrow. "I have never taken a lover, mate, or husband. I..." She considered telling him of her royal identity, how she fought against his ancestor many years ago. She considered also telling him that her mother was a goddess, and that she had inherited some of Aldorin's divine power. But a sharpness in her gut warned her to remain silent. She bit the inside of her cheek.

The prince smiled, ignoring her pause. He seemed to only hear she'd not yet settled for any man or beast, and he questioned her no further about her past. His expression was now readable; he was confident he'd ensnared her.

Nadia's chest tightened.

"I must admit, last night I was not myself. If you'll have me, I would very much like to court you, Nadia." He kept a few steps between them, his hands relaxed at his sides. "I want you to feel at ease here in Arioch, to grow accustomed to life aboveground, to regain your strength, and learn about our kingdom. I want to do things properly." His gaze caught hers, steady and deliberate. "But no one must ever discover who you truly are. Our laws forbid magical creatures, save for those of the Perri duchy, from serving the throne. I need you to understand the risk I'm taking... the risk I'm *willing* to take to keep you safe."

Nadia's heart kicked against her ribs like a trapped bird. She heard him—his confession, his desire—but also the *truth*, harsh and undeniable: her curses had worked. What she had feared was true—none of her people were here.

She felt it all at once, like the air was stolen from her lungs. The absence of magic.

She felt empty, hollow. The warm tea had offered her a phantom feeling of what magic could really do to strengthen her *eluviam*, her magical center. She understood now, with a parchedness, that human sustenance could never replenish her starving magical core. She lived hundreds of years in darkness, so she hadn't noticed when her magic had depleted to nothing. The curses she cast over the years had gradually eaten away at her. Drained her.

Before she allowed her thoughts to spiral further, her gaze flickered to Azriel's. He'd asked her to keep her identity secret. He was waiting for her to comply. Did she have a choice? Her throat bobbed as she replied, "Yes, Your Highness. I won't allow such a thing to happen."

His lips curled into a grin, and he reached into his robe to retrieve a thin oval-shaped disc marbled with color. He held it out for her. "Then please eat one of these elixirs daily. They will conceal your pointed ears and sharp front teeth. They will make you appear human." At her hesitation, he gingerly grasped her

wrist and closed her fingers around the elixir. "Eat this, then meet me in the dining hall for breakfast. I'm loath to see you in such a skeletal state for much longer."

With these last words, he hurried from the room, shutting the doors behind him.

Nadia fell to her knees, her strength gone. Fresh tears stained her cheeks. Her body shook, mourning the loss of a part of herself she'd never planned on giving up. Perhaps the prince had stained her goodness with his cruel smile, or maybe he'd convinced her for a moment that his love was pure and true. Even if his affections were dishonest or ill-intended, she couldn't bring herself to refuse his kindness. Not after he helped her escape. Not after he gave her a chance to see the sun again.

She *had* to believe him. But her body knew better... It wasn't love that curdled in her stomach, but a spoiled hatred. A sickening revulsion for what she had done.

When the elixir melted on her tongue and the colors of the room melted together until all she could see was black, something cold burrowed within her. There *had* been magic there, a very small amount. She reached for it blindly, the warmth flickering.

Before she could grasp it, the cold stamped it out.

# VI

# DISCOVERY

Lady Karmin Kittel watched with a prickle of annoyance as Prince Azriel excused her chaperone, Lady Bernadette Ferle—whom Karmin had grown quite fond of since her arrival at the castle—and took her behind a row of thick trees.

He'd *finally* deigned to meet with her. She hoped he had a proper explanation for his dismissive behavior in his rooms.

Karmin stood opposite the prince and clicked her tongue, feigning disinterest.

The Morathan noblewoman found the crown prince of Arioch to be equally as attractive as he was overbearing. He had never been subtle about his judgment of her character—she found herself both drawn to his honesty and repulsed by his self-obsession.

Before she could utter a word on her own behalf, he told her he would formally refuse the marriage proposed by King Augustus and King Ordyr, because he had already given himself to another woman, body and heart alike.

Of course, he hadn't stated it in such lyrical terms.

He regarded her with dark eyes that said *you're not worth my time,* and she realized her hopes of his feelings developing for her during their time apart were in vain. He visited her at last, not out of curiosity, but because he wished to explain himself honestly before refusing her hand.

"Neither of us was ever attracted to the other." The crown prince sighed. "You wouldn't want a husband who must playact his affections, would you?"

Karmin pressed her tongue to the roof of her mouth to keep from saying something she might regret. She almost told him women were never granted the choice he was brashly making, but she knew he already understood that. The gleam in his eyes told her he wasn't trying to help her—he was only helping himself.

*Selfish, ignorant prince.*

She would be dumb to continue to find him diverting, knowing his true character. So, dumb she was, for his lack of interest stoked her desire to capture his attention even more.

When she first met him, she was just a girl—awkward, self-focused, not at all mentally prepared to begin referring to herself as *spoken for*. Still, when she'd caught sight of him at fourteen, she was infatuated by his confidence. During their brief introduction, however, she sensed he thought her little more than a child—he showed no interest in learning about her, in speaking with her, in even pretending to care who she was. But she knew something he did not: she had been told from a young age that their fates were bound. Even with her frailty, she was destined to inherit his kingdom, bear the next heir of greatness.

She held onto that promise as though her life depended on it. As far as she knew, it did.

"Your Highness," Karmin said. Azriel regarded her warily. "I have spent my entire life preparing to be your wife. This is not a matter of attraction. I cannot afford such a luxury. If you are concerned I might take offense should you keep a lover, rest assured, I will not. My duty is to give you an heir, nothing more. You may share your bed with whomever you wish. I will not be offended—"

"I wish to make *her* my queen." The weight of his words silenced her. They were so final, so commanding.

Her heart thumped in her throat. Jealousy pricked behind her eyes. How she *wished* to be the object of such directed affection and protection...

"I shall be your queen in name only, Your Majesty." Karmin would not yield. Not yet.

Just behind Azriel's large body, Lady Bernadette was pacing through the trees. Her blue skirts swished noisily against the brush.

Karmin hoped her friend could hear their conversation, so she could comfort her later knowing all that had been said.

"I don't want you." Azriel's jaw stiffened. His eyes held no warmth.

Karmin composed herself and forced a smile. Her eyes moistened, but she knew better than to appear shaken by his words. To show her true feelings would mean she'd no longer be taken seriously. She hoped he would hear her. If only he would *hear* her.

"That will not be an issue." She stepped toward him. Lucky for her, his body was aligned with a thick birch tree. "I will be a strong, suitable queen for you." Another step. His back hit the tree and a glow of something like panic lit his eyes.

Karmin reveled, her teeth catching her lower lip to keep her smile hidden.

"You are ill. You will die young. You are the definition of all that is *weak*." This time, his voice shook.

The first crack in his armor.

"I am *strong*," she countered. "And when I am gone, because you *are* aware I will perish prematurely, I will leave behind a mighty son for you. He will inherit our strength. And he will serve you well."

He blinked at her. The clouds cleared from his eyes, and for a second he might have *seen* her. Her sincerity, her honesty.

She clung to his expression, memorized it. Her longing increased—to be seen with such genuine curiosity... She never wanted him to look at anyone else the same..

"If that is all," she said with a click of her tongue, "I will return to accompany my friend, Lady Ferle." Karmin lifted her eyebrows and angled her head toward where Lady Bernadette awaited her, just behind him. He blinked at her, and his face morphed back into its unreadable state.

She brushed past him, pretending not to feel the energizing warmth that flooded her when her bare arm touched his robes.

Tea. Karmin wasn't fond of it unless it was cooled first. A foreign ambassador had introduced the alternate method of drinking it, and she much preferred hers iced. In Morath, her family understood her peculiar preference, but here in Arioch, would requesting it prepared in such a way offend the prince? Would her presence, meant to symbolize peace between their kingdoms, instead provoke war?

She curled a finger through her teacup's handle, stroking the warm porcelain with her knuckle. Her conversation with the prince had gone better than she expected, yet uncertainty still lingered. What if he decided to send her home, the fragile alliance between their kingdoms shattering because of their failed union?

The thought excited her as much as it terrified her.

Lady Bernadette tapped her finger lightly on the small tea table, and Karmin snapped her attention to her friend's face.

Bernadette had always been kind to her. Years ago, when Karmin was visited by the crown prince, Bernadette accompanied him. Karmin had assumed the lady was there to judge her worth and capabilities as the future queen. Karmin *had* been only fourteen and knew little of what was required of Azriel's betrothed. Bernadette was nearly ten years her senior, recently come to adulthood and unmarried. She must have been brought along for another reason, but Karmin never thought to ask.

And she would not. It mattered little why Bernadette had accompanied the king-to-be, only that the lady had been undeservingly kind to her. Karmin swallowed that kindness desperately, as if it were water from the purest of springs.

Karmin considered them to be friends, exchanging letters in the many years they didn't see each other. Bernadette was still unwed, and a wrinkle was beginning to form between her brows, but her expression was still soft, warm. Because Karmin was still young, she preferred her friend's company, believing it inappropriate to be alone in a foreign land. Bernadette was the perfect age to be both chaperone and confidante.

When Karmin arrived the day before, the lady welcomed her with a hug and seemed grossly interested in what had transpired over the past few years in Morath, as Karmin rarely wrote about political affairs in her letters. The lady looked at her now with a look of concern.

"Do you not care for spiced tea?" Bernadette asked.

Karmin touched the rim of her porcelain cup. It was beginning to cool, but she knew she wouldn't be able to hide her true feelings about the drink if she sipped while it was too warm. She was loath to see Bernadette's reaction to her strange preference.

"On the contrary." Karmin smiled. "I quite enjoy spiced tea. I am merely lost in thought."

Bernadette lifted her cup to her lips and sipped daintily. Her gray eyes peered over the rim, as though saying, "Would you care to share what you're thinking about? You know I'd love to hear anything you have to say."

So, of course, Karmin unwound her lips and told her friend everything.

She tried to ease her friend in with how she felt about hot tea. But she couldn't suppress how she felt toward the crown prince. She told Bernadette what he had said to her in the garden. And, most painfully, she told her of the precious little time she had remaining. That was what weighed on her most.

Bernadette reached a hand across the small table and clasped Karmin's, gripping her fingers with a bony sincerity.

"Mere...*months*, my lady?" Bernadette seemed short of breath.

"Of course, if I refrain from overstraining myself, it could be much longer. The physician was unsure." Karmin shrugged. Bernadette's fingers tightened.

"We will have the royal physician do an assessment. If you are to produce an heir, you will need to last longer than half a year." At Karmin's wilted expression, Bernadette reached her other hand across the table to cup Karmin's. "Of course, you are worth much more than your womb, my lady. I apologize. I must confess, I am simply and utterly at a loss for words. We certainly need you to be seen by our physician."

Karmin let out a brittle laugh. She detested the pity in Bernadette's eyes. Hated that all anyone could see in her was weakness.

"Of course," was all she said. A clipped response. Bernadette straightened, her hands retreating to her cup.

Then, clearing her throat, Bernadette lifted a small bell from the table and shook it twice, the shrill clang of metal summoning the servants to clear their tea. When a stout maid arrived, Bernadette held out her arm. The maid looked puzzled, but Bernadette simply shook her head. "Bring a tray of ice for Lady Karmin," she said. "She takes her tea as His Highness does."

AT NIGHT, Karmin wandered the halls of Arioch's grand castle. No, *her* castle. It would be one day, despite the crown prince's grumbling. Her spirits on the matter were gradually returning.

She slept her first few nights in the king's bedchamber, where King Augustus promised she'd consummate her marriage with his son. But Azriel never appeared there during the night, not after that first day when he'd dismissed her—embarrassing her before she could step fully into the light.

Instead of sleeping, she explored the castle halls with a pricket and candle to light her way. She took her time admiring long corridors plastered with busts of previous kings, all akin to one another but never in quite the same way as the last. Some had the same nose, while others shared the same eyes. Most had facial hair, but Azriel's would surpass them all once a portraitist captured his essence. The black of his beard seemed to trace back to the kingdom's first ruler, Arioch Faundor. Of all the kings, Azriel looked most similar to this ancestral king.

Arioch held a tradition that would not allow any face save for the kings' to be painted. No prince's face graced the walls until he ascended his father's throne.

It was a horrible waste to wait to paint such a handsome heir.

She let her thoughts wander, picturing the crown prince, too large for the throne, settling into it with an air of intimidation while a royal painter strove to capture his magnificence.

Her heart pounded in her ears. Warmth fluttered down her spine.

She pulled herself away from the wall of portraits and continued, her candlelight flickering uneasily as she continued down

the hall. Her heartbeat steadily thrummed, interrupting her delirious thoughts of the crown prince.

When her body cooled and her heart settled, she could tell something was wrong, for the throbbing sound lingered. It had transitioned to a steady pounding. It didn't take her long to realize the sound was no longer her own heart, but something else striking the same relentless rhythm.

She craned her neck around the corner and spotted a pair of doors, slightly ajar. Above them, bronze dragons twisted around one another—Myrn and Steil, the legendary dragon gods of Arioch. Karmin knew their significance well, for they were integral to the kingdom's strength. Legend held that these ancient dragons still lived, producing offspring every fifty years, each hatchling born stronger than the last. The young dragon would be set against the next crown prince in a trial to determine whether he was worthy to inherit the kingdom. And the dragon's heart, she had read, promised strength and longevity to whoever consumed it.

Karmin had been expected to learn much about Arioch's customs and traditions, and of them all, this was her least favorite.

She stepped through the doors into a vast, empty ballroom. Chandeliers hung high above, their crystals catching the moonlight streaming through the tall windows. The pounding sound echoed through the room, sharp and insistent. Karmin followed it to a side door, cracked just enough to reveal a sliver of shadow within.

Karmin hesitated. Who could be inside? Or *what*? Was she about to discover something that would traumatize her? She shook her head. She knew it wouldn't matter—she was prepared for far worse than mere fright. For her entire life, she was to be ready for death at any turn.

With a breath, she held a hand to her flitting heart. She could do this—monsters didn't exist, and even if they did, Arioch had strict laws against them. Nothing behind this door would harm her.

She slid her fingers along the wood, then pulled the door open. Inside was a modest, empty room with no windows and cold, tile flooring.

Sitting cross-legged at the room's center was a small woman with hair as dark as night and skin as pale as the moon. Karmin's candlelight kissed her form, making her seem to glow, like a diamond catching the faintest spark.

Karmin's hand shook. Who was this woman? A ghost? She didn't believe in such things, but what else could explain what she saw now? Arioch may have outlawed beasts, but did this extend to the paranormal?

The pounding stopped.

The woman's hands were raw and bloody, pressed against a crooked tile with a blunted corner now stained red.

Bile rose in Karmin's throat.

The pale beauty cocked her head, a dazed look in her pale eyes. Karmin froze, afraid she truly *was* a ghost, and that any slight movement might agitate the spirit.

Then the woman looked at the mess she created and smiled. "Oh." She coughed, then lifted her hands, exposing her palms for Karmin to examine. The blood gleamed, still dripping from her palms, but...

Karmin blinked.

She took one of the woman's wrists and flattened her hand.

"This doesn't make any sense," Karmin muttered.

The woman smiled weakly.

Karmin's eyebrows furrowed. The woman bore no wound, but she'd certainly bled. What kind of sorcery was this?

"I cannot harm myself. Not for long, at least," the woman explained. Karmin met her eyes, and saw a sudden ferocity there.

It was a feeling she knew well—self-hatred. But something else accompanied it.

"Why were you trying to?"

The woman shrugged and cradled her hands. The blood stains spattered her white nightgown. "I had a vision."

Visions were another thing Karmin did not believe in. They were only reflections of what people wanted to see come true. Desires, wicked or good, cloaked as *divine revelation*. She only trusted prophecies foretold by witches, those who predicted her fated marriage to the prince of Arioch.

"Was the vision so painful that you had to harm yourself to forget it?"

The woman laughed. The sound was foreign to Karmin, non-human. Perfect. Confusing. Haunting. Karmin's head spun as though under a spell.

"I've longed to die for many years," the woman said. Her hands pulled her knees to her chest and she buried her face in them. "My goddess has shown me a time to come where my child will suffer greatly, and die by his brother's hand."

"A son?" Karmin asked. She hadn't considered it before, but a woman with this kind of beauty could be exactly the kind of person the crown prince fell for. But if this was so, how could he let her wander off to hurt herself?

She was no lady, no noble. Karmin was unsure *what* this woman was. But she exuded an ancientness, something Karmin couldn't place. The longer she stood in her presence, Karmin almost felt compelled to show respect, as if the woman were, herself, divine.

The woman nodded, and a crystalline tear slipped from her eye. "A prophecy. Once the king is crowned, he will receive the same prophecy from a group of witches. Seers. I was shown the prophecy earlier, a... a blessing from my heavenly mother."

Karmin held her breath. The woman could be lying, yet the

chill in her words told Karmin otherwise. She had to be telling the truth. Karmin felt she had no choice but to accept it.

"I thought taking my own life would be the answer, but my blood is too pure. Too connected to the goddess. I can wound myself, but my skin seals before the pain has time to settle. I may no longer be able to use magic, yet my blood still carries the power of my holy mother. I cannot die by my own hand."

Karmin held her breath. She was unsure what the woman could mean—was she claiming to be the daughter of a true goddess? Her image was ethereal, true, but her actions and words were that of a demented mind.

"You would..." Karmin's lips quivered. "You would take your own life to prevent harm coming to your unborn child?"

"Would you *not*?" The woman's voice grew agitated.

Karmin smiled thinly. "You do not know me. I was told my entire life that my days are numbered, that I have no chance to live long enough to even *bear* a child, and here you sit, claiming you'd steal the life from your unborn son just to save yourself the pain and torment of knowing his future." The woman seemed stunned, but Karmin pressed on. "If my child was prophesied to die, to kill his own father, to run away, to kill me, or to drown himself, I wouldn't care. I would still give birth to him. And I would die doing it."

Silence filled the room. Karmin knew she sounded desperate, foolish even, but she didn't care. Her only desire was to be the mother of the kingdom's heir. Her illness would have to wait.

"I admire you."

Karmin snapped her attention to the woman. There was no mockery in her voice—only sincerity. It unsettled Karmin, the way this woman who didn't know her situation seemed to see straight through her.

"You jest," Karmin huffed.

"You are courageous. You would choose to have the child, give it a chance regardless of what fate predicts. That is brave." The woman rubbed her hands together, flakes of dried blood crumbling to the floor. "I have wanted to die for a long time, but seeing your determination... it makes me want to reconsider." She paused, then added softly, "My name is Nadia."

"Karmin." She scrutinized Nadia, wondering why she didn't include her familial name in her introduction. She purposely omitted hers as well.

"Would you do something for me, Karmin?"

Karmin stared at her. After a moment, she huffed. "I will not kill you, if that is what you shall ask of me."

Nadia laughed, this time with more warmth. "Of course not. I should like for you to scribe the prophecy for me. I wish to keep it, to protect my future son. He deserves to know his fate."

This wasn't what Karmin thought Nadia would request of her, but it seemed simple enough. She nodded. Nadia's face relaxed.

"I will retrieve a quill and ink." Karmin backed away to the door, holding the candle steady. "Meet me in the library, and I will write down that which haunts you."

# VII

# PROMISE

Nadia's vision was vivid in her memory. She wished she could wipe it away—smear it, change it—but she knew better than to wish such things. Aldorin's visions were divine, true... Fate dictated. She couldn't stop what was to happen...but perhaps she could delay it.

Nadia prayed to her heavenly mother, begged her. Aldorin was the divine counterpart of her parentage, only speaking to Nadia when she deemed it necessary. In the past thousand years, Nadia's mother had been utterly silent. Which was why the goddess's sudden voice in Nadia's thoughts both angered her and gave her hope, even when the truth revealed to her was anything but.

It was all she could do to hope fate could be changed, or, at the very least, postponed. Her heart yearned for the smallest chance that things could be different.

Nadia pulled herself to her feet, dusted the remaining blood from her hands on her thin nightgown, and left the abandoned ballroom. The prince was asleep in the chamber she shared with him. He hadn't noticed when she left the night before, and she doubted he would notice her absence tonight either.

With a steady breath, Nadia padded on bare feet to the large library, which was rather far from the prince's quarters. The candle Karmin held in hand meant she was as curious about the castle as Nadia was, but the elf queen's reason behind her curiosity wasn't as purely willed. While Karmin held a genuine interest in the castle because she would soon live there, Nadia searched for places to hide and escape.

It took Nadia a bit of effort to wrench the library's tall oak doors open. They were heavy, usually operated by guards, so she did not have the physique required. She was persistent, regardless. She focused on one door, pushing it with all her back, her heels digging into the floor. This did the trick.

Once Nadia was inside, she peered around. Karmin had not yet arrived, so Nadia searched for a place to wait without disturbing the stacks of books and oddly placed tables of whoever studied there during the day.

The library was dark, but a few tall windows cast moonlight over empty desks and chairs. She settled onto a curved windowsill, wide enough to fit her small body comfortably. The moon wasn't quite yet full, or maybe it was waning. She breathed a sigh of admiration. The stars bowed to the crescent light, winking at her like they knew something she didn't. But she held as much knowledge—the vision crept into her memory like a disease.

Behind her, the doors to the library scraped open. Karmin grunted, and the doors clicked shut. The small light from her candle did little to illuminate the room, but it brought out the red tones of the woman's chestnut-colored hair. She was small, with a round face and slanted eyes. Quite pretty. Nadia could sense the woman didn't realize it.

"Blasted door," the lady cursed. Then, "Come, before we are discovered."

Nadia slipped from the windowsill and approached Karmin, who had begun spreading writing materials over a mahogany desk. A quill pen, a pot of ink, and a few wrinkled pages of parchment, scarcely larger than either of their slender hands. But it was all Nadia needed— a small note, something to hide in secret. Anything larger, and she would be putting both of them at risk.

Karmin set her silver pricket down last, the candle quivering in a pool of warm wax. The light snapped and crackled, then steadied, obedient.

"What will you have me write?" Karmin seemed out of breath, but Nadia heard the excitement in her question.

Nadia breathed deeply, wetted her lips, and recited the prophecy she'd witnessed. Her heart grew heavy as she spoke, each word growing quieter than the previous. She didn't have to repeat herself—Karmin was quite quick with her hand, her letters swooping and beautiful. Nadia couldn't read the written language of Arioch, so she had Karmin read it back to her for accuracy.

Karmin cleared her throat, then repeated Nadia word for word.

*"In Arioch 'tis reasoned, a prophecy foretold,*
*A tarnished Faundor son, a destiny bold.*
*Appraising the throne, his father's life to sever,*
*He'll reign with vengeance, his fortune's endeavor.*

*"Born of darkness, his identity concealed,*
*He'll gather allies, his power revealed.*
*With sword in hand, and facing father's might,*
*He'll take his rightful throne, ushering justice and light."*

The words were eerie, final, and felt impossibly more damning when spoken from the mouth of another.

Karmin, too, seemed shocked by the revelation. Her eyes became clouded, as though viewing an alternate reality, the words themselves cursing her to speechlessness.

Nadia hurried to warn Karmin of the potential consequences

of sharing the prophecy, reaching for the young lady's hand. Karmin flinched away from her touch, but the haziness drained from her gaze when she refocused on the elf queen.

"It is the first and last time I am able to speak this prophecy aloud. It must be your first and last time, too," Nadia said. Her voice was raspy, resisting the curse beginning to take hold. One of the only curses that was older than her, and not her own doing.

"Why is that?" Karmin asked. Her voice also took on a hoarseness. She seemed surprised by how rapidly it was changing. Her hand went to her throat and her eyebrows pulled together.

"A person can only speak it once aloud, a curse to prevent circulation. If you try to recite it again, the curse will steal your voice forever." Nadia's words strengthened as she spoke, the curse's warning dissipating.

Karmin's eyes lit with understanding. She nodded gravely.

"I will keep this note safe." Nadia folded the parchment neatly, careful not to smudge the ink, and slid it underneath the thin fabric on her shoulder. "I know we've just met, but I trust you won't spread this secret."

Karmin mumbled something. Then, a little louder, she said, "Will I see you around the castle often?" Her voice had an edge to it, but Nadia didn't think it was a lack of faith.

"It's likely. But I don't plan to stay for long," the elf queen said.

Karmin straightened. "Will you leave?"

"I do not belong here, as I'm sure you've realized. But I'll need your help if I'm to leave this place."

She watched as Karmin entwined her fingers together, her eyes exposing her eagerness to help Nadia escape.

She was beginning to understand Karmin's uneasiness—the prospect of marrying the future king must have weighed heavily on her mind, and Nadia appeared to be standing in her way. For a moment, Nadia considered telling her about the crown prince's professed affection, but decided against it. She wanted nothing more than to leave as soon as she could. Telling Karmin would only do more harm than good, and they were hardly friends.

"There is a welcome ball, I hear." Karmin spoke slowly. "I'm sure all attending will find themselves preoccupied with the festivities to take notice should you decide to slip away. It's happening in a fortnight. Will that be soon enough for you?"

Nadia grasped Karmin's hands and laughed. All those years in the dungeon, and her freedom was *this* close. Someone was not only willing, but *excited* to help her leave.

She didn't care *who* this woman was, nor if her intentions were selfish. Not when Nadia's freedom hung in the balance.

Oh, if she could kiss the envious young lady.

Nadia's thoughts wandered toward what she would do once she returned to her people, even down to the details of her death. She wished to be slain by one of her own, in a respectable way. A sacrifice, as it suited her—sent back to her heavenly mother.

Before she could get too ahead of herself, she said, "That's perfect, Karmin. I will forever be in your debt."

Karmin wrested her hands from Nadia's grip and smiled tightly. "Do not thank me yet. I promise to help you, and in return, I wish to never see you again. This prophecy... it is evil. I felt it as the words rolled off my tongue." The lady shook her head, and brownish red hair tumbled over her shoulders. She grimaced. "I am stricken with guilt. I detest that I agreed to record it for you. I... detest you more for making me recite it. You deceived me."

"I apologize," Nadia said. She meant it, but she also didn't regret asking Karmin to speak the prophecy aloud. She could not leave the spreading of it to chance. "But I suspect you would have done the same if you were in my position."

Karmin ground her teeth together, but she said nothing. Nadia took her silence as agreement.

The two parted with unspoken understanding. After they shoved the doors open again, Nadia watched Karmin leave the library with the quill, ink, and extra sheets of parchment bundled under her arm. Once Karmin was far down the hall, Nadia slipped away as quietly as she could, stepping lightly until she reached the prince's chambers.

Azriel slumbered, his bare chest rising and falling slowly. She slid under the covers, shivering against his warmth. She scolded herself for finding comfort in it, telling herself it was the heat alone she appreciated. His fascination with her might be fleeting, and if she could leave soon, he would have to soon forget her.

He was young. It was not love he felt for her, but intrigue, obsession. She may have briefly believed she could love him because he rescued her, but the feeling fled as quickly as it had come.

She sent a second prayer to Aldorin, though it was more a plea for her own sake: that all would proceed as she hoped, that Azriel would take no drastic actions before the ball.

Nadia had a sinking feeling Aldorin would be deaf to this prayer as well.

# VIII

# PLANS

During the weeks leading up to the ball, Azriel was busy attending strategy meetings and making plans for foreign guests. Nadia rarely saw him, and when she did, she made herself scarce. If he spotted her, he was terribly obvious about his desire for her—he had a habit of angling his body to face her, his eyes burning with longing.

He was inconsistent in where he slept, and it kept Nadia awake at night. Some evenings, she wished she could wrap herself in the thick window curtains so his heaviness would not disturb her rest when she least expected it. She made her boundaries clear, and he generally respected them. He wished to lie beside her, and nothing more. Yet something about this puzzled Nadia. Was he acting out of respect, or was he scheming something greater? On their first night together, he had lost control. Granted, she had too, but she never would again. He *could*, though, and she did not know if her weak body would be able to resist against him.

A week before the ball, he sank into the mattress, flung an arm over her shoulders, and pulled her into him. Her body was tiny, and fit the curve of his torso. His arm was tethered with muscle and tense. Any resistance would injure her, so she didn't attempt to move.

She thought about Karmin. The lady was often seen in the gardens. There was a lightness about her that Nadia knew came from their deal. They hadn't spoken since the night they met, and that silence ruffled her. Nadia feared Karmin might grow reckless and expose their plan to Azriel. The two seemed to be growing close, too... or, at least, Nadia let herself hope so. It would make deceiving him that much easier.

"Have you selected a gown for the ball?" Azriel's words muffled sleepily into her neck.

She tensed, her throat bobbed, and she nodded stiffly. "One of the plain ones."

He shook his head, groggy but persistent. "I told you before you'll be on my arm the entire evening. You need to look my match."

"I've been eating well, thanks to you," she offered. "Is my improved complexion not sufficient?"

He chuckled, though she could tell he was losing lucidity. "Yes, my dear."

Nadia felt her face go hot at the sudden warmth in his voice. He called her by her name most nights, but now, the endearment was different. Her heart dropped.

She didn't respond. His breathing mellowed and he drifted to sleep. She hoped he would forget what he said.

Eventually, she fell asleep too. But she awoke throughout the night, looking at the window for the first sign of daylight. She decided to search for Karmin and discuss their plans for her escape as soon as dawn broke. They didn't have much time left, and Nadia's unease was growing.

The fourth time she woke, the sky had turned to shades of rust and deep violet, the horizon bruised with the yawning sun. Azriel was gone, his side of the bed left in disarray. Nadia slipped from the sheets, dressed herself in the blue and gold robes she'd been fitted for, and stepped into the corridor. The hall was quiet, save for a few darkly cloaked figures standing at intervals along the wall. They were always there come morning, and she had learned to ignore them. They made no move to stop her as she hastened toward the king's chambers, where Karmin slept.

During the past week, Nadia learned why Karmin was at the castle. She was betrothed to Azriel from a young age, soon to be queen. She was dignified, kind, and wished to protect what was hers—she was the perfect candidate. Nadia tried to ward off the guilt plaguing her... Sharing her bed with a man promised to another was ill-fitted to her conscience, but she had to remind herself it was also not her choice whether he joined her or not.

For a fleeting moment, she pondered telling Karmin. But if the queen-to-be learned of the prince's nightly visits, everything might fall apart. She could not risk it. Not when her freedom was so near.

Nadia didn't knock. The doors opened easily, and she entered the room without hesitation. Karmin was still asleep, her breathing slow beneath the tangled sheets. Nadia hesitated only a moment before calling her name.

"Karmin."

The woman stirred, then sat with a groggy scowl. "Nadia. To what do I owe the pleasure?"

The elf queen knelt. She spoke fast, keeping her voice low. "You know."

Karmin sighed, her tongue pushing into her cheek. A look of annoyance crossed her, quickly replaced with smugness. Nadia didn't let it affect her. "Of course. The plan. But it's hardly appropriate to approach me in such a way. You *do* know whose room you've entered, do you not?"

Nadia nodded. "You're Azriel's betrothed."

Karmin ground her teeth. "You've found out. So why do you continue to share his bed?"

Nadia worked her jaw, then her eyes flicked away. Shame

shook her entire body. She chewed on her inner cheek to help distract the discomfort curdling in her stomach.

Karmin *knew*.

"I have no choice."

"I know." Karmin's jaw ticked. "He tends to be like that. Do not worry yourself, I don't hold it against you." She tucked a reddish brown strand of hair behind her ear. "I *try* not to, at least."

Nadia bowed her head. "I am eager to discuss how I may safely escape. I wish to flee the prince's side as earnestly as you wish to join it."

Karmin was silent for a moment, then cleared her throat. "Not here," she said at last. "Tonight. In the garden. My friend, Lady Bernadette, shall explain the details."

"Thank you." Nadia's eyes moistened.

"Again," Karmin said, her voice a hum of agitation, "do not thank me. Not yet."

"I must thank you for your willingness to help me, despite everything."

Karmin clicked her tongue. "Leave, but let no one discover you have visited me. Should anyone question you, say you lost your way."

Nadia bowed once more, then left the room. The corridor was empty, but she felt the hush of the castle press in, reminding her that one misstep could undo everything.

ROUTINE WAS SETTLING UPON NADIA. Breakfast was served by royal cooks, and she dined alone most mornings save for the punctual arrival of the prince's white-haired advisor. Without fault, he came each day to ensure she ate one of the bitter elixirs to conceal her elven features. Gradually, her body grew less susceptible to the initial effects of the magical disc—she no longer fainted upon consuming it—though a lingering sickness still gripped her briefly each time she ate one.

She wondered what would happen if others discovered her true identity. The advisor seemed to know who she was already, and even though he didn't like her very much, she could tell he held his tongue around her. His posture remained defensive, as though if she were to make one wrong move, he would be ready to strike. To him, she was a threat.

She didn't take offense at this.

After he left, Nadia would spend her days in the library nook, letting the sun warm her. She liked her new routine of taking long, slothful naps there. No one noticed her, and even if they did, they never questioned her catlike presence. This was how she reclaimed the sleep stolen from her when Azriel paid her sporadic nightly visits.

Each time she would wake from her nap, she found herself gazing at the library, daydreaming. Her fast-approaching escape gave her hope, and that hope played across her memory in all of its potential forms: she imagined greeting her people, telling them what had happened to her, and, conversely, she imagined pretending to be a normal elven woman, having escaped from the castle. What would her life look like before she surrendered it at last?

Tonight, she would learn of the plan that would help see these fantasies realized.

When dusk colored the sky with its orange tint and the sun retired for the night, Nadia stretched her limbs and stopped by the kitchens for an apple, then bounded toward the garden. She couldn't seem to get there quick enough.

The halls were silent, almost eerily so, but she paid them no mind—she had only one thing on which she was capable of focusing her attention tonight.

The gardens were breathtaking, bathed in moonlight. Though there was no magic in the castle, the bugs that flitted around lazily, emitting an occasional yellowish light, were a sort of magical oddity on their own. Nadia was unsure if she had ever seen such insects... If she did, she certainly would have remembered them.

The dayblooms were shut for the night, but the nighttime flowers yawned before the risen moon, arching their stems to fully face the heavens. Most of these flowers were milky, a shadow of the brilliant reds and yellows of the daytime plants.

Nadia's heart twanged.

These flowers, while beautiful, would never reach their full potential without the sustenance of the goddess's magic. As she walked past a group of pale blue blossoms, the scent wafting alluringly into her nostrils, tears budded in her eyes.

These were Aldorin flowers. Named after the goddess herself.

Without magic, they were steadily withering away, desperate to soak in their last moments of blessed moonlight before they perished.

Nadia's skin prickled with cold, even though the warmth of day hadn't quite yet left the air.

Lady Bernadette was a dot of burgundy in the dark, knees forming a tent with her dress as she splayed a book across her legs. Her eyes squinted tightly at the text as though she were intensely concentrating on the book's contents.

Nadia wondered if the young woman could read without much light, or if she was taking a gamble on the flickering creatures whizzing lazily about.

The elf queen tried to get closer without disturbing the woman, but even with her light steps, the lady seemed to notice her. She snapped her book shut with a hand, cleared her throat, then pulled herself upright and gracefully smoothed the layers of her noble dress.

"You look lovely, Miss Nadia," the lady said. Her voice was light, airy, but sweet as well. Her gray eyes traveled quickly over the simple clothes Nadia wore, and she smiled. "The future king seems to already favor you a great amount. Are you sure you're set on leaving so soon?"

Nadia wondered at how the hideous combination of gold and blue she wore could possibly communicate Azriel's fondness, but she supposed being fitted for it ought to have raised a few questions.

The years were beginning to weigh on the elf queen—she was forgetting the trivialities of courtesan etiquette and the meanings of certain colors. When she ruled in Aldorin, she never cared for such things, but elven women had often approached her with requests for blessings and wisdom in marriage. By association, she needed to have a basic knowledge of human traditions.

This was, of course, more than one thousand years ago. Arioch now was nothing like she remembered, and customs must have changed as well.

She did not belong here.

Nadia sighed.

Bernadette raised her brows, prompting the elf queen to respond.

"It is the one thing I wish for, severely." Nadia's words came out hushed—Bernadette might not have heard her if it weren't for the way the lady's nose pinched and lips puckered.

"I will not question your decision, Miss Nadia. I only ask for you to consider a potential life here at the castle, and compare that to a life beyond its protected walls." Bernadette turned, weaving through vines weighted with dark berries. She looked back, beckoning Nadia to follow. "You *are* aware of the state of the kingdom?"

"I suppose I am not." Nadia fell in line with Bernadette. The noblewoman's dress made her appear at least thrice the size of the elf queen, the skirts flouncing around her like ripples in a pond.

Bernadette nodded, clasping her hands behind her back. She tipped her chin to the sky and a solemn smile rested naturally on her face. The maturity in the lines around her eyes disarmed Nadia. Surely a woman centuries younger than Nadia could not withhold so much burdening knowledge, but the depth of Bernadette's gaze made the elf queen unsure.

"You need not hide with me, Miss Nadia. I am aware you are an elf, despite the fairy magic you eat each day. I know far too much concerning His Highness's fascination with you, starting from years ago when he found you in that cell, and even before then, when His Majesty forbade anyone to enter the dungeons, claiming them to be devoid of life and empty. He wanted to continue a reign of peace, you see, so he saw no need to imprison anyone. But there were always rumors..." The lady tapped her chin, then sighed. "My apologies, I am getting off topic. Aldorin, the forest where your people reside, has been neglected for years. Laws affect those within the *human* boundary of Arioch. That is, if anyone from the enchanted forest were to leave and be spotted, they would be brought and enslaved or executed for entering His Majesty's dominion without permission."

Nadia held her breath. Her people *had* been exiled, then. For how long, she did not know. But why would the elves be allowed to live at all, if they were confined to the borders of their forest, where they were useless to the king?

The elf queen knew the answer, and it both steadied and frightened her.

Aldorin. Her heavenly mother and the goddess of the forest. Often silent, but ever-sovereign. She sheltered her children as long as they remained beneath her boughs. The human kings must have tried to overtake the forest, and failed.

Nadia couldn't think of any other reason why her people would be let alone, pressed to the far reaches of the kingdom.

"You know much," was all Nadia said.

Bernadette laughed. "As do you. Though age seems to be far kinder to you."

Nadia humored the lady, laying an arm in front of her. The pale skin, smooth and unblemished, was like the marble of a freshly carved bust. "Immortality is appealing until you possess it, I am afraid."

It was Nadia's first confession of her true self, she realized. She felt a prick of panic, but it subsided quickly with the soft edges of Bernadette's knowing smile. A warm energy swirled about the lady, one Nadia felt she could trust.

"I can only imagine how it must feel to never age, to feel trapped in a life and forced to watch everyone you love pass away while you alone continue to live." Bernadette continued walking and Nadia followed. She was growing more and more curious about Bernadette's thoughts on her situation. "I think it would be rather lonely."

"Yes." Nadia's words were empty. She did not know what it was like to lose people over years. She certainly didn't consider the kings she saw in passing as anyone to mourn. Instead, she was haunted by the memory of the war, the day she lost her soldiers, the day she lost a good friend. When she considered the possibility of boasting many friends throughout her long life, her stomach turned with despair.

They reached the end of a path and turned to go down another. This one was lined with rose bushes, but the flowers had already closed, guarded by abrasive bushes of dark.

"I am to go with you." Bernadette's voice was scarcely above a whisper. "Lady Karmin managed to convince a merchant who came with her from Morath to retrieve her dowry on the night of the ball instead of the next fortnight. We will travel with him in an Ariochan supply wagon."

As simple as that, the plan was spoken at last. It took Nadia a moment to process the details, and when she finally did, nausea rose like a tide within her. Had freedom ever been so easily won? No, surely the prince's eyes would find her—he circled her every step like a hawk waiting to engorge on its prey. He would never let her out of his sight.

She supposed she would have to figure out how to excuse herself from the ball, since it was not a part of the grand scheme. And then she would have to gather anything she wished to bring with her, even though she had little aside from the gifts she received from the prince, and—

*Wait.*

"You are... coming with me?" Nadia's mouth twitched. She could not discern why the lady would go with her. Unless... Bernadette also wished to escape?

"Yes, Miss Nadia. We shall treat it as business for the queen-to-be. It would seem more strange if you left alone. You see, matters of court are determined by rank. Lady Karmin must wield her authority over you to affirm her place as the king's intended. His Highness may be momentarily enraged, but he will understand she is only reminding you of your station. More importantly, he won't be able to do or say much about the matter." Bernadette smiled. "Once married, a king's wife has power and control over his consorts. And that is what you are to be, if you ever return." Bernadette reached across and cupped Nadia's hand. "You understand, yes?"

Nadia nodded. Bernadette's explanations were plain enough for her to understand, but the implications of her status should she return struck her with fear.

"I do not plan on coming back." Her skin crawled.

Bernadette squeezed her hand once, then released it. "No, I don't think you do either. But you must consider what your life would become, should such misfortune come to pass."

Nadia was struck with a silence that made her body shiver. A stillness, an icy despair she hadn't acknowledged before.

The prophecy... It promised her a *royal* son.

She had to keep her distance. She could not allow it to come true.

Bernadette grunted, then faced Nadia. Her eyes were pale and wide. "The night of the ball, after your first dance with the king, excuse yourself to reapply powder. But before you turn the hall toward the guest rooms, escape through the servants' quarters and meet me near the stables. There is a shortcut through the kitchens. I should already be waiting for you, but if I am not, you must not let the driver leave until I arrive."

Nadia arched a brow. Was this not a sensitive mission? What would happen if she was discovered hovering around the stables, alone?

Bernadette laughed softly. "Do not worry. Should they find you, say you were misled—or drawn astray. Let your time in the dungeon shoulder the blame for your confusion. The prince will believe you, as blue and gold have ever been his colors."

Nadia blinked. "His... colors?"

"Oh, not officially, no." Bernadette's smile was wry. "But in truth, he has always taken pride in the finery he keeps close. Whenever a woman caught his fancy, he would gift her with gold and blue tapestries, bedding, gowns. He claims the colors signify worth and beauty. Dreadful taste, truly. Oh, but I have likely spoken too freely." Bernadette seemed, least of all, ashamed of her opinions. Nadia couldn't stop the grin lifting her lips.

"You have said just enough." Nadia nearly laughed, and the feeling of it in her throat surprised her. It had been long since she found anything humorous, but maybe there was hope for her yet.

Bernadette returned her smile. "I think you and I will get along just fine. Lady Karmin worried for nothing."

"She does not hide her distaste for me," Nadia said.

Bernadette seemed surprised by the elf queen's observation. Nadia was also confused as to why she had voiced such an opinion. But Bernadette had this charm, this *effect* that made Nadia want to reveal centuries of suppressed emotions. She did not worry that the lady would judge her for speaking her mind.

"Quite the opposite, Miss Nadia," Bernadette said. "It is a shame you are positioned as enemies, but she will help you get what you seek. It is the least she can do for you, since you are also giving her exactly what she desires."

Nadia smiled, but her eyebrows knitted together as her thoughts churned. The queen-to-be was a confusing creature, saying one thing and thinking another. But to hear her hostility was only for show warmed Nadia in a way she knew not how to interpret.

"You *do* know what she desires, yes?" The question was intoned more as an assumption.

Nadia finally allowed herself to laugh, though it sounded rough, forced. "What else?" Bernadette's stoic expression begged her to elaborate. Nadia wetted her lips. "The crown prince, of course."

Bernadette nodded and looked away. "A pity, that girl. I'm afraid she has always wanted what she shouldn't."

# IX

# ESCAPE

The day of the ball arrived, and Nadia could not still her nerves. In the nights leading up to the ball,, Azriel had stayed away from her bed—a mercy, though it did little to ease the torment she felt, knowing she would be bound to him for the evening. Worse still, she feared her plan to escape might fail entirely.

The day passed as usual, though everywhere she looked, servants bustled through the halls with bejeweled foreign trunks and carts of wine. Guests arrived sporadically during the day and would linger for several nights after the ball, their feasting expected to continue into the following week. Nadia overheard that the only other time so many foreigners were invited was during the Feast of Undying, a duel named after the war her people lost, meant to crown the new king.

Nadia ate alone the entire day. In between meals, she was too wracked with worry to rest in her usual spot in the library, so she took to wandering the grounds. In her gold and blue, no one questioned her presence—she could do anything she wanted to and no one would bat an eye. She was the prince's pet.

The blue and gold looked horrendous on her. The dark blue clashed with her midnight hair, and the reflective gold made her skin look impossibly more pale. She seldom cared much about the clothing she wore, but this combination she abhorred.

Her nerves led her back to the prince's bedchamber, and when she arrived, maids awaited her, arms laden with tulle and lace. Nadia nearly cringed at the sight of those same cursed colors. She hadn't imagined her humiliation could take a new shape, yet here it was, draped in silk and lace.

"His Highness had this gown tailored specially for you, Miss Nadia," one of the younger maids announced. The rest of the servants followed an unspoken command to hang the dress over a folded partition, then they returned to Nadia, flanking her on all sides.

They pulled her clothes off and ushered her behind the partition. Nadia guessed the faux wall was a formality for the ball, since they never bothered to help her change before, and they all just saw her naked, but she said nothing.

They were quick with their work, gingerly pushing her thin arms through long sleeves and cinching her waist with a stiff corset. She was already petite, so she didn't understand why such measures needed to be taken, but she supposed lifting her breasts would give her the illusion of having a fuller, healthier figure, so she held her tongue.

When they finished, her hair was meticulously curled atop her head, her lips colored a deep rouge, and her eyes lined with cobalt kohl. Nadia gaped at herself in the looking glass, hardly recognizing herself. She looked... *human.*

A tremor shot through her.

She had never longed to be human, never thought it was even an option for her. She was born into her queenship, blessed by the goddess. She was the *last* person who could pivot and choose a different path, but... seeing herself now, she was beginning to envy a life of mortal innocence, a terminal life like Bernadette's. It was a beautiful thing, impermanence.

The feeling tugged at her, toyed with her. For a moment, she allowed it, admiring the youthful face reflected in the mirror.

The light in her eyes scared her. So she banished the hope before it could take root.

She had other plans. She already made her decision.

"The ballroom is ready to welcome guests," a familiar voice called at the door—it was not the voice Nadia wished to hear. The silver-haired duke poked his head in, squinting his eyes at Nadia. With venom, he asked, "Have you eaten the elixir today?"

The maids pretended not to listen, their expressions carefully blank. Nadia nodded, unsettled by his question. If her identity were truly a crime, and Bernadette had spoken the truth, why risk exposing her in front of the servants?

"You're to enter as soon as you are dressed. His Highness is not a patient man, and he's expressed a great desire to announce your...*courting* in front of the nobility." The man seemed to choke on the word, as if the mere concept of her relationship with the prince disgusted him.

Nadia bit the inside of her cheek. "I'll be there soon."

"No," he interrupted. "I am to see your safe arrival. You will have many eyes on you tonight, both from allies and enemies. I have been instructed not to let you out of my sight."

Nadia smiled, imagining how Karmin might respond in such a situation. Would the lady speak biting words and tilt her nose so she was looking down its slope at the duke? Or would she blink slowly so her dark eyelashes shaded the sparkle in her eyes as she told him she would do what she pleases, and he wouldn't be able to do anything about it? Nadia wasn't as practiced at faking, but she decided to try her best.

"Very well. Ladies," she addressed the maids. "Are we done here?"

They said nothing, just bowed then left the room, keeping their heads lowered until out of sight.

Nadia cocked her head at the duke, and he grimaced.

"Blue and gold usually *complement* Azriel's romantic exploits," he mumbled. But he would not have said it if he hadn't wanted Nadia to hear. And, as an elf, her hearing was impeccable. He knew that too.

Nadia felt a burning in her chest. She wasn't sure what this man held against her, but she felt a strange resentment toward him. Not because he forced her to take her elixirs every day. Not even because he never formally introduced himself. No, because he seemed to genuinely hate her. Each time he spoke to her or looked in her direction, it was as if he were about to vomit, his face contorting together, tinged slightly green—the mere thought of being near her unbearable.

Bernadette had called him a *fairy*. Could he truly be a fairy? And if he was, why did he hate her so? She had been allied with his ancestor!

Confusion curdled in Nadia's stomach, hurt warring across her features. What could have happened in the last thousand years for him to foster such deep hostility toward her? Did all fairies bear such animosity? Or was it just him? New questions formed, but she didn't think he would answer even if she asked. He knew she was an elf, but as far as she was aware, she had only told Bernadette of her immortal nature.

The duke grumbled before he offered her a hand. Pale, like hers. Slightly gray in color.

Nadia settled her fingers in his palm and he visibly shivered.

"No need to force yourself," she said.

He squeezed her hand in response. "Do not speak to me as if you could understand."

Nadia swallowed. She didn't know what to say in response, or if she *should* say anything.

"Come with me. Let's get this over with."

THE SPACIOUS MAIN ballroom swarmed with noblemen and women, bursts of color swirling to the hum of stringed instruments. Faces were already flushed with drink, and couples stood too close to one another. Candlelight was abundant, brightening the room from tables, wall sconces, and the crystal chandeliers twinkling above.

The moment Nadia and the duke arrived, he released her arm and disappeared. He had been right—the second he deposited her, all eyes were trained on her, grazing over her like she was a shiny new statue to be erected in place of the beautiful three-tiered fountain at the center of the room. Some guests watched her with admiration, others with confusion or disgust.

She walked past, her soft shoes padding lightly on the hard ground. Noblewomen flicked fans over their faces, concealing gossip. But their eyes told all—the intrigue, the envy, the curiosity.

Karmin stood among a group of women near a wall of exquisite—albeit grotesque—paintings depicting war. Nadia's stomach dropped when she neared them and saw exactly *what* was being depicted among the bloodshed: elves, fairies, creatures, all dead save for the human king in gold armor standing victorious above them all.

The future queen either didn't seem to notice, or was entirely unaffected by the horrendous illustrations.

Karmin spotted Nadia and made a point to turn away so as not to call even the slightest attention to their involvement with one another.

Nadia expected this, but somehow, she felt the rejection as if it were real. Karmin had never given her reason to desire a friendship, but Bernadette had planted something in Nadia that gave her hope. If Bernadette hadn't told the elf queen that Karmin liked her, she might have taken this act of blatant disregard as dislike.

Karman was a brilliant actress, Nadia realized.

A servant rushed past Nadia with a large silver tray boasting gilded goblets of blood-red wine. She swept one into her long fingers and pressed the rim to her lips. The burn in her throat and the bitter edge soothed her, distracting her from her emotions.

Tonight was not about such frivolous things as friendships and pleasantries. She would escape, and if everything went well, she would never return.

Hope swelled in her anew. She could hardly wait to dismiss herself and slip away to the cart awaiting her.

"You look dashing tonight, Miss Nadia."

*There* was the familiar voice Nadia had been wishing to hear.

"As do you, Lady Bernadette," Nadia replied. They curtsied at one another.

Bernadette smiled brightly, the silver in her brown hair a natural ornament to the gray and blue dress she wore. It was an off-shoulder confection with lace that covered her bosom and choked her neck. It had the timeless elegance Nadia wished had been reflected in her own gown, but hers was designed for a younger, smaller body.

Nadia did not afford herself the feeling of embarrassment. If all went to plan, she would remove the dress long before the night ended. Burn it, even.

"Might I introduce you to a few of the court ladies?" Bernadette's voice was guarded, less familiar. But Nadia knew she had to play along.

"Of course."

The lady inclined her head and smiled, her gray eyes vacant. She wove through the guests, making introductions for Nadia. In less than an hour, most of the hall was acquainted with the strange beauty dressed in black hair, white skin, and most notable of all, the crown prince's preferred colors.

They were bowing to a gaggle of girls when the king's entrance was announced and the music stopped, bodies froze, and the room fell to a sudden silence.

King Augustus was haggard, his beard turning white, but his dark eyes were fierce and vengeful. If *this* was the picture of peace, Nadia struggled to believe what a modern tyrant would look like. Augustus bore the spite of Arioch, the same oppressive body, the same ire in the slant of his mouth. But maybe appearances alone were not enough to define a man.

The king sat on his throne. Two smaller thrones flanked him, and they were quickly filled by two older women. One wore a crown, the other a veil.

"Welcome to Arioch." King Augustus's voice was loud, but weakened by age. The rattle in his words sent a hush over the guests. "We are pleased to honor Lady Karmin Kittle of Morath tonight, as well as her imminent betrothal to my son, Azriel, for the purpose of uniting the beautiful kingdoms of Morath and Arioch."

Smattered applause. Mutterings.

Karmin stepped forward and raised a hand gloved in pale pink silk. Her smile was charming, her eyes caramel in the excessive candlelight.

"And now, I shall announce the arrival of my son, your future king, Azriel Faundor."

More applause, though this time it was more raucous.

The crown prince appeared from a side door, dressed in military refinery. His robes were gold, maroon, and black—Arioch's colors. A silver circlet sat on his curly black hair. His beard was finely trimmed, shaping his square face with a severity that commanded the attention of the room. His underclothing—tunic and belt and boots—was all black. Against the splashes of color in the room, he was shadow incarnate.

He loomed momentarily, dark eyes searching the crowd. When his gaze snagged on Nadia, he moved with purpose toward her.

The whispers rose, a hissing tide that pushed the crowd back. Silk fans snapped open, shielding faces and masking mouths. Bernadette was gone. Nadia stood at the center of the dance floor, the sudden, violent weight of her isolation pressing in from all sides.

When Azriel stopped in front of her and bowed deeply, King Augustus shot from his seat.

"What is the meaning of this?"

Azriel merely raised a hand.

"Your betrothed is to be your first dance, Azriel!" The king's voice was filled with rage and far more power than it had moments before.

Azriel lowered his hand. His attention flicked purposefully to Karmin, then returned to Nadia. A grin spread over his lips, and a flush deepened his cheeks.

"So it shall be." His voice was so quiet, even Nadia with her elven hearing almost missed what was said. He turned to the orchestra sitting to their right and nodded.

The violins shrieked and cellos bellowed to a slow, suggestive waltz. The prince scooped Nadia into his arms, a hand firm against the dip in her back and the other loosely holding her wrist.

Nadia did not know how to dance, not like how humans did, but Azriel made it terribly easy. He moved her as though she were a flimsy doll he was used to practicing with or a feather he twirled between two fingers. He knew the steps, so she simply needed to relax and let him fling her about.

She didn't heed the stares, couldn't bring herself to glance in

Karmin's direction. This was not her doing, and she desperately hoped Karmin understood that.

As Azriel spun her around, Nadia emptied her thoughts. The buzz of wine flowed through her, and the rush of air calmed her. She enjoyed the moment, even though she didn't care for the man holding her. Anything could feel pleasant if her freedom was the result of it.

When the violins faded into another song and the rest of the guests joined in, Azriel gripped her hand and pulled her to the dais. He didn't seem to care when she winced under his sudden forceful grasp.

"Father," he said. King Augustus frowned. "This is Nadia. She is who I would like to wed, not Karmin. Though if the lady must stay, she will be made a royal consort and held in high regard, as Lilith is to you—"

Nadia didn't process the blow that cut across Azriel's cheek until after it had already happened, and the prince was rubbing his jaw.

The room continued their dance, oblivious (or ignorant) to what was happening.

"You could have said no." Azriel chuckled. There was no mirth in it.

"I thought I did," said the king. With a cough, he turned to the veiled woman and clasped her hand as though to comfort her. "You *will* wed Karmin, and that is final. The treaties have been signed and dispatched to Morath. The ceremony shall take place in a triduum, once the welcome festivities have ended."

"Father," Azriel growled. He gripped Nadia's hand harder and pulled her into his side so she bent awkwardly and groaned. "She bears my child. Do you refuse her still?"

Nadia felt her chest tighten at the falseness of his reason. Her cheeks flared with shame.

She wished to protest, but the king did so before she could utter a word.

"Blasphemy!"

The women on either side of the monarch touched each of his arms to settle him. His breathing had grown ragged.

Everyone was slowly shifting their attention to the quarrel. The music continued to play, but heads were angled conspicuously at them. Ears pricked in interest.

Nadia wanted to disappear.

*And soon, I shall,* she promised herself.

"I took her to bed," Azriel snarled. "If she births a son, *he* is to be the rightful heir."

"Be gone." The king's voice was weak. "You have committed a great disrespect to our guests. I will not—"

Azriel raised his voice, forcing the music to stop. "I *will* wed this woman. *She* is to be my future queen." He turned to address the guests. A proud smile whipped his features into a contortion of victory. "I demand respect from *all* of you for my decision."

More whispers.

Nadia dared to scour the room. All eyes were trained on them, most glassy with shock. Karmin stood, her arms crossed and her face tight. She didn't glare at Nadia, though. She aimed her disdain at the prince.

"Take me to my rooms," the king said. The queen and the king's consort helped him stand, and a line of servants followed them out. The room was quiet until they were gone.

Azriel snagged a goblet of wine from a stationary servant, then raised it.

"Drink much, dance long, and have a splendid party. My mood has much improved now that the brute is retired." He drank three long gulps and gasped with pleasure.

The mingling bubbled up once more. The musicians resumed their bouncy tune.

Everything returned to normal.

Nadia realized she hadn't said anything, and if she didn't soon, she would lose her only opportunity to, so she entwined her fingers with his and rested her cheek on his shoulder. Her skin crawled, but by his reaction, he didn't seem to notice how uncomfortable she was.

"Your Highness." Nadia tilted her head, her voice dropping to a melodic silk.

His eyes glinted with hunger. "Yes, my love?"

She hid a grimace by tightening her lips into a painful smile. "I am afraid all this attention has made me rather flustered. Would you allow me to stop by the washroom to powder myself before we are to dance the rest of the night?"

Azriel pulled her closer, a grin tugging his features. In a low grumble, he said, "You are offering to dance with me all night?"

Nadia coughed and masked it with laughter. "Who else would dance with a promised woman?"

Azriel nodded in approval, then released her. The second his hand left her, she felt as if she could fly, freedom only a breath away.

With a deep curtsy, she smiled and walked at as normal a pace as she could manage. She even paused by certain groups of nobles to establish her casualness. She gave polite greetings, then turned from the ballroom.

Washroom. If there was such a place, she didn't know where it was. Or couldn't remember.

When she reached the kitchens, which were empty save for the dish washer who hummed a dissonant tune, she nearly squealed in anticipation.

She slinked past, bunching her skirts in fists as she made for the stables.

All servants were either eating their evening mess, sleeping early, or attending to the nobility in the ballroom. No soul graced the halls she whisked down, no soldier was there to stop her.

Things were going very smoothly, almost to a fault.

Hope stirred within her, the future she dreamed of just beyond her reach. She flew past the stablehand who snoozed in a chair outside the horse stables. The smell of hay filled the air, sweet and earthy. Nadia circled the building anxiously, expecting to see Bernadette and a wagon waiting for her outside.

She found a carriage instead, its windows darkened.

Nadia's heart stuttered and her feet skidded to a stop.

In the driver's seat sat a familiar silver-haired noble. When he turned to look at her, she noted the mask he wore to conceal the lower half of his face. His anonymity confused her, especially since his hair gave away who he was.

She found herself caught in indecision—to feign ignorance, or to turn and run.

"Good evening. I told the Morathan man to leave early. But do not fret," he said. His voice took on a sardonic edge. "I will gladly see you delivered to your proper place."

Bernadette arrived soon after Nadia, but she was much less surprised by the switch of their driver. In fact, she almost seemed to expect the change.

"Viktor, you wouldn't dream of exposing this ruse to His Highness, would you, dear?" She spoke with a familiarity that seemed almost doting, as a mother might speak to her child. But she couldn't have been more than a few years older than the fairy duke. Bernadette continued to intrigue Nadia.

The duke snorted. "She wishes to leave, and I want her gone, so our wishes align. Telling Azriel would bring her right back to him, would it not?"

Bernadette laughed. "You are a smart boy. Now, shall we go?"

She reached over and touched Nadia's shoulder, hope flickering in her eyes as she ushered her into the carriage. Bernadette settled across from her. Once the door was shut, she released a sigh that seemed to carry years of burdens and old grudges with it.

In an instant, Bernadette seemed younger. Nadia wasn't sure if she was imagining it, but the wrinkles around the lady's eyes and mouth softened, and the gray in her hair darkened, blending seamlessly with the rest. She also wore a loose tunic and trousers now, which made her look rather daring.

She held Nadia's hands in her own and gave them a gentle squeeze.

"Home."A sly smile spread sleepily over the lady's lips. "Let's get you home."

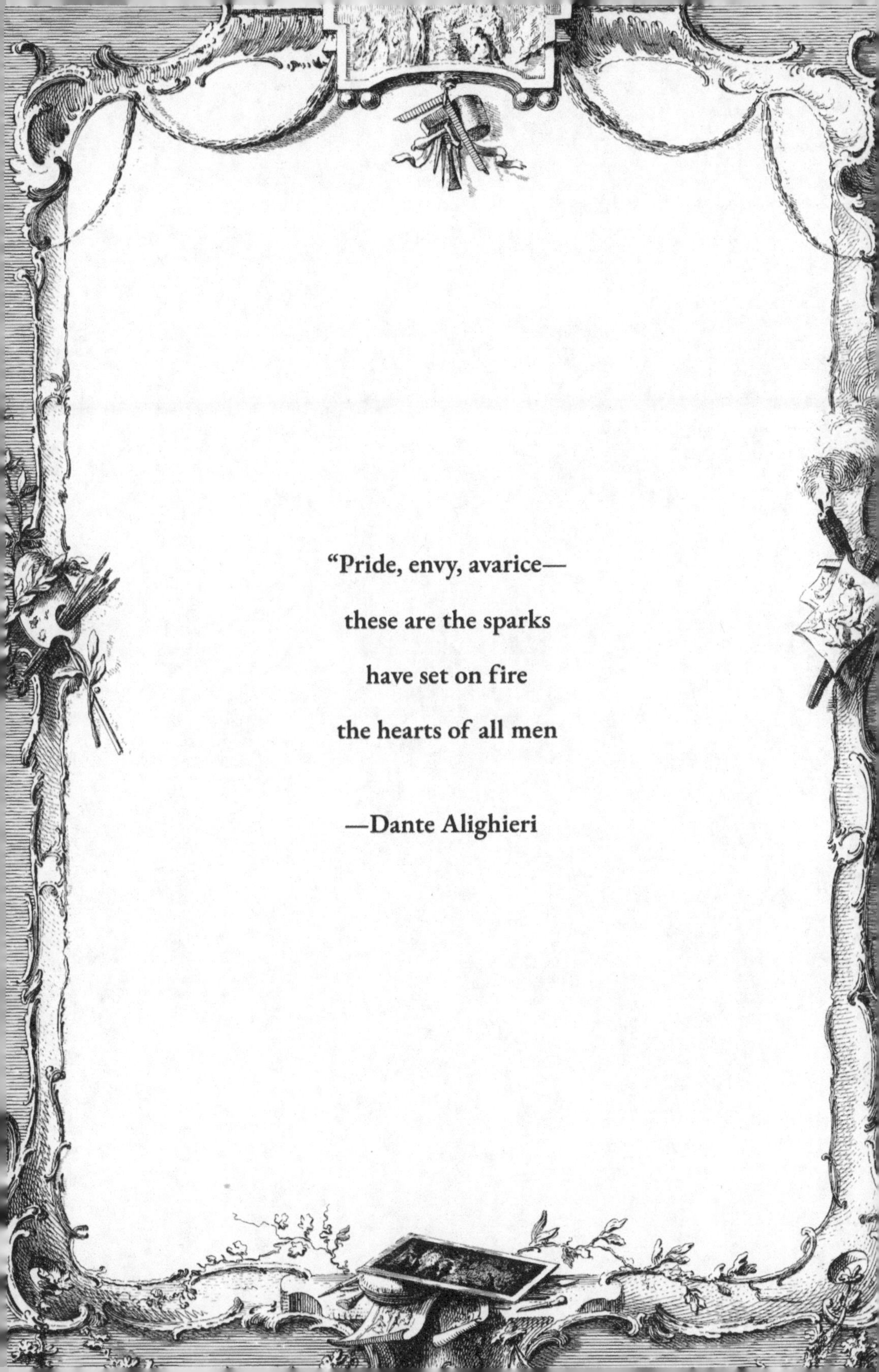

"Pride, envy, avarice—

these are the sparks

have set on fire

the hearts of all men

—Dante Alighieri

# X
# SURPRISE

SEVEN YEARS LATER

Arioch was his home, his kingdom, his inheritance. And yet, even though he would be crowned king and given all he was promised in a short few hours, his stomach roiled with anxiety and anger.

His wife, the royal princess Karmin, had failed to produce an heir in the time they'd been together, but it was no fault of hers. They rarely shared the same bed, and when they did, it was only under the pressing insistence of King Augustus.

Karmin was slumbering behind him in the grand king's bed. Last night had been one of the few they spent together during their five years of marriage. He looked over his bare shoulder. A soft smile rested on her lips.

Azriel was beginning to grow fond of his wife, perhaps because she kept her distance, yet remained perfectly available to him whenever he called on her. Karmin's condition didn't seem to be worsening, but Azriel knew better than to trust her practiced smile. She was growing thinner, her spiteful personality subtly softening at the edges.

The prince stood at the large window, surveying the large courtyard below. Servants clipped hedges with sharpened hand-blades, having conversations he could not hear. He wondered for a moment if they were gossiping about him. Most servants used to grow quiet in his presence, but now he scarcely heard a word from them—they had their conversations where they knew he wouldn't hear them.

He turned from the window and glared at the stone ground.

"You're awake?"

Azriel didn't react to the sleepiness in his wife's voice. He folded his arms over his bare chest and continued to scrutinize the old flooring.

Karmin yawned, then appeared at his side, slipping an arm around his waist. She rested her head against his shoulder.

"You called her name again," she said. "Last night."

Azriel's jaw tensed, but he did not look at her.

"It's been seven years, Az. I don't think she will return."

He harshly shook her off and turned to his wardrobe. Then he lied to her. "My thoughts are far from that woman. You ought to know where my concerns lay this day."

"Of course." There was a smile in her words. "Your coronation duel. Do you feel well prepared?"

Azriel grunted.

Karmin knew he was masking his grief for Nadia, but saying so would cripple his authority. In this way, his wife would be a brilliant queen. She held her head high and made a habit out of confidently challenging him in ways no one had before.

But now was not the time.

"I've trained my entire life to confront Steil's hatchling. If I were ill-equipped, my entire lineage would suffer for it, my name a blemish on the kingdom's record."

"Defeat the dragon, then, and you can officially make me your queen."

"Yes." He lied again, but this time he felt he was more convincing.

"You know you will be the first I alert if I discover I am with child." Karmin reached a hand to Azriel's back and pressed it against his skin.

He shuddered, and her hand fell away. "Who else would you tell first?" His voice was stony. "Go wash yourself. I need time alone to prepare."

She disappeared into the washroom wordlessly.

A single knock sounded on his chamber doors. Azriel reached into his wardrobe and grabbed a thin robe, shot his arms through the sleeves and tied it at his waist.

"Enter," he said.

A head of almost-white hair poked into the room, followed by the lanky body of the Perri duke.

"Have you come to collect me, Viktor?"

"Indeed, Your Highness."

Their relationship had been stagnant for the last decade, neither overstepping nor ignorant of the other. They were ineluctably connected to one another, for reasons Azriel felt cowed to admit—tied together by an ancient oath-binding magic. Viktor, with all his status and bravado, would always be the prince's subordinate. At one point, Azriel relished the superiority and power he held over the duke's head. Now, he was weary of encountering the agitated fairy anywhere he went.

They stared at each other for a moment, both understanding the weight the day would carry. Not only would Azriel face a fearsome mythical beast, he would also be crowned king upon his victory. Thankfully, the nobility seemed to favor him, and if his father's immediate decision to abdicate was any indicator, he seemed to have no doubts about Azriel's success, either.

Viktor bowed stiffly, averting his gaze first.

As he should.

Azriel puffed his chest and glanced at the door. "Escort me to the armory."

Viktor straightened, nodded, and turned. The prince followed him down long hallways and up spiral stairwells to the very top of the castle's west tower. The armory was unguarded at the top, especially on a day like today. Privacy was tradition, and other than his wife, no one was to see or touch him until he was in the arena. Viktor was the only exception as his aide and confidant.

The room was decorated with reflective metal that hung from large hooks in the walls. Dark blades, crescent moon scythes and short daggers glimmered under the light of the early afternoon sun. Each pristine, crafted by the royal blacksmith of Arioch, Mavis Brimvelde. The renowned and reclusive artisan never showed his face, and only appeared during the year of the new king's coronation. He used enchanted materials to form the blades, crafting weaponry that served as perfect vessels for magic. More tradition now than tool.

Azriel flexed his hand, then reached for a gilded broadsword. Viktor rushed to his side, nodding his approval.

"An excellent choice, Your Highness."

Azriel studied the blade in his palm, turning it in the light. It certainly was impressive craftsmanship, but he didn't want to pick something with such haste. He returned the sword to its hooks and took a step away to observe other weapons.

Viktor followed him closely, his dark eyes giving away nothing. Each weapon Azriel plucked from the wall received nods of approval from the duke.

After checking the fifth blade—a curved scimitar with a leather-wrapped handle—Azriel cleared his throat.

"Has my armor been prepared?"

"Yes, Your Highness."

"Bring it here."

Viktor bowed, then traveled across the room to the wall of armored statues. He knelt at the base of the wall to open a large wood chest, and he began removing large pieces of mail and plate armor.

Azriel scanned the wall of weapons one last time, and his eyes snagged on the broadsword. After touching the enchanted metal of so many pristine blades, the sword seemed to have a gravitas the others did not. It was...*his* sword, the one that would slay the dragon, he was certain.

He retrieved the sword, laying it flat on the circular bench in the center of the room.

Viktor brought each piece of armor to the prince. Azriel secured the chest plate, the gauntlets, the plackart, and his leg pieces while his aide configured the smaller pieces.

"How is Felicita?" Azriel found himself asking. It was unlike him to show interest in Viktor's private affairs, but once he wore the crown, he would need to master the art of feigned concern. It was a small pittance to pay a man bound to the throne until his last breath.

The duke paused his work, blinked at Azriel, then pressed his lips together. Years ago, the duke had hoped for a son, even proclaimed his wife bore one, but he now had three daughters.

"My wife is well," he said. "We are still hoping for a son. The next child will be our last. We will pray to Arioch for his blessing on our family in return for our continued loyalty to the throne."

Azriel nodded. He didn't know what else to say. The conversation was stale to begin with, so he allowed silence to swamp them. Viktor continued fastening pieces of the armor together, his eyes squinting in concentration.

When Azriel was fully outfitted, he bent his neck so Viktor could fit the helmet over his head. The visor snapped shut over his face, but the low visibility was nothing new to him. Fighting wars across the land had required him to don similar armor, and he had fought thousands of enemy soldiers. This time, he had but one adversary. There was no comparison.

Azriel lifted the sword and wrapped his metal fingers around the grip, then slid the blade gently into the sheath strapped to his waist. He breathed, and the metal expanded with him, as if the armor itself was alive. Lightweight and fitted perfectly to his body.

"Best of luck, Your Highness." Viktor bowed deeply as Azriel grunted and left the armory.

King Augustus's mages awaited him, cloaked in black. They were the private council to the throne, offering priceless knowledge and insights on the creatures of the wood. It was gradually becoming tradition for the curious cloaked figures to escort future kings to their coronation duels.

"Frederick, Michael." Azriel greeted them. They angled their heads down, their milky white eyes the only visible portion of their faces—the rest was covered with so much white cloth, the structures of their faces were obscured.

"Your Highness," they both spoke at once. The tether between the mages fascinated Azriel. They were still each unique, but they shared one voice. "The crowd awaits your arrival. We wish to congratulate you beforehand on your victory."

Azriel puffed his chest.

Viktor finally entered the hall, bowing briefly in reverence to the mages. He was to take up the rear, sword at the waist. No one would dare attack them while they traveled to the arena, but such precautions were tradition.

The mages turned, then led Azriel down the tower's stairwell, across crenellated walls, and into the castle training grounds. The arena was an oppressive structure made of stone that angled into the ground. The seating encircling it was crowded with nobility, barrels of beer attended by servants every few yards.

The crowd bustled, laughing and chattering about as they waited for the event to begin. Azriel looked toward the arena's dais, where the old king sat high above. His white beard had grown long, but thin. He rarely left his bed, and anyone would be able to see how death closely attended him. The gods must have kept him alive for this moment, the time for Arioch to see a new king crowned. The paleness of Augustus's skin might have shocked Azriel if it weren't for his hatred for him. He was glad his father would abdicate today. He would have enjoyed it if Augustus had done so years ago, but ever since Azriel's insubordination at Karmin's welcome ball, Augustus had hardened himself to the idea of letting Azriel reign any sooner than was necessary. He had even forced Azriel to remain at the castle while Nadia was disappeared, insisting a prince shan't run after "some peasant girl." For seven long years, he was unable to search for her himself.

Now, at last, Azriel had the chance to right his father's wrong.

The mages stopped at the arena's entrance, and the crowd quieted, acknowledging Azriel's arrival. King Augustus was announcing something, his voice tired and frail. His coughs, which interrupted him, were louder than his words.

A hand fell on Azriel's shoulder, the sound of flesh against metal making him cringe.

It was Viktor. The look he gave Azriel was indiscernible, but the prince saw no animosity in it. There was something deeper, more complex. *Later*, that look said. He would tell Azriel whatever he had to say once he was crowned king. Like with many of the kingdom's secrets, he must have one that could only be revealed to him once he was sitting on the throne.

With a stiff nod, Azriel turned and stood between the mages. Each bowed to him, then turned to face the arena.

Neither said a thing, for they had already expressed their confidence in him. This would be over quickly. The anticipation knotting in his chest was a phantom of the pressure he may have felt if he were much younger. Now that he was in his thirties, he had no stomach for surprises, and preferred to know the outcome of things before they began.

When he stepped into the arena, he knew immediately this would be a quick victory.

The hatchling was a shackled thing, quivering in its chains. It had Myrn's colors—orange and purple, splotchy and random. Steil's black was absent. If the legends of the mated dragons proved correct, this hatchling would be weak like its father, not strong like its mother.

The way it cowered when Azriel advanced disappointed him. To these mighty creatures, the prince should have seemed much smaller, hardly a threat. And yet, this one seemed to only want its parents, small round eyes frantically flicking around in search of their comfort.

The hatchling was thrice Azriel's size, but this was considered very small for a dragon.

He almost pitied it.

"Begin," Augustus called, his voice brittle. The crowd roared at last, no longer able to hold their excitement.

Azriel turned to the gallery, opening his arms wide to display his armor. He was impressive, and it was his duty to showcase how formidable he was. He thudded a fist to his chest, a dull sound ringing out. He did this again and again, and the crowd caught on quickly. Applause gradually built, increasing the frequency between claps until their support crashed all around him.

Finally, Azriel turned on the beast. Its wide, black eyes blinked rapidly, searching the sky for an escape. But its wings had been strapped to its spine for this fight. If the poor creature hadn't gained its spark yet, this would be an even quicker battle than Azriel imagined.

Four armored guards flanked the dragon, removing the iron

muzzle from its maw before they unlocked the chains roping its limbs to the stadium walls.

Once it was free, it immediately pressed itself against the perimeter, trying desperately to cover itself with its wings. But, tied as they were, it was unable to protect its head.

Azriel unsheathed his sword, admiring how the black blade glittered in the sun. He held it in one hand, not sure he would need the precision of both arms to end the beast's life.

"The only thing standing between me and the throne...is you," Azriel purred. The beast blinked, turning its head downward.

The prince approached until he stood a few feet away. He raised the blade, ready to plunge it through the creature's skull. He brought it down quickly, and—

The dragon darted out of sight.

Azriel whipped around, and the beast was at the center of the arena, sitting on its hindlegs. Its claws cracked the ground beneath it.

"That's more like it." A grin tugged at his lips. He would have been disappointed if the duel was too easy, but he still knew it would be over soon. The dragon lacked confidence. It continued looking around frantically for its parents. Lost. Afraid.

The prince rushed the colorful creature, knocking it over with nothing but a heavy shove to its side. It scrambled, trying to right itself.

The crowd cheered, jovial. Beer spilled from glasses clashing mid-air.

"I don't suppose you have any fire? Or are you still too young?" Azriel spoke so quietly, he was sure only the dragon could hear him.

Its dark eyes blinked slowly, and for the shortest amount of time, Azriel thought he saw an emotion there—glassy, wet.

Then the dragon pulled itself up, its scales sparkling. The hatchling shook violently, and it opened its jaw the tiniest bit.

A spark spiraled from its throat and popped in the air. Then, nothing.

The dragon looked ashamed.

Azriel laughed, but bitter disappointment settled in his gut.

How had he let such a pitiful fight drag on so long? Had he really intended to give the dragon a chance? Why? He was wasting precious time. The crown on his father's head belonged to *him*. He had no reason to cater to the beast's pitiful existence.

The crowd watched in anticipation as Azriel flicked the sword to his side.

"Enough." Disgust coated his tongue. "I will now send you to join your siblings in the cosmos."

One sweep was all it took. The blade swooshed through the dragon's throat, separating its head from its body in a clean arc. Dark blood emptied from the beast, its head rolling a few feet before it stopped, its eyes open but vacant.

The gallery was louder than ever, somehow satiated by this pathetic display of power. Azriel was discomfited by how easy it had been. How could he have taken the life of such a weak, underdeveloped creature? But he would not let the guilt get to him. Winning was winning, and the crown was now his.

That was all that mattered.

In his books on legends, it was said each dragon's heart bore immense power to whoever consumed it, yet Azriel found himself disgusted by the thought. Such a weak dragon couldn't possibly harbor a strong heart, and he did not delight in the idea of eating it raw. So, with a decisive turn away from the dragon, he puffed his chest and met his father's leveling gaze.

King Augustus loomed above on the dais. Azriel bent to one knee and angled his head. Behind him, servants were already dragging the beast's corpse away.

"Father, I have defeated the offspring of Myrn and Steil, the symbols of our land. I will now graciously receive your crown and inherit the kingdom you have stewarded, as our ancestors have done for centuries." The recitation was fresh on the prince's tongue. It felt right. In that moment, he forgot about the dead beast and the crowd around him. Nothing mattered except the power of the crown and the freedom it would give him.

"Rise," his father said. Azriel could barely hear the command, but he stood obediently.

Azriel's mother—the queen, Candace Faundor—stood at the king's side and bowed, then carefully removed the regal crown from her husband's head. At the same time, Viktor rushed into the arena and helped Azriel remove his helmet. The circlet he usually wore was with his mother, and she would give it to Augustus during his final years of life before it was eventually passed down to Azriel's heir.

A mage approached the queen and received the crown with a bow. The king watched warily as the mage descended the steps and into the arena, crown steady in its white hands.

The queen readied Azriel's circlet, simple and decorated with thin leaves of silver. She waited, her expression unreadable from where her son stood.

It was then Azriel noticed Karmin, standing to his mother's side. She was dressed in a regal gown. Not blue and gold, as she preferred lighter colors. The yellow of the fabric contrasted beautifully with her dark curled hair.

The mage finally arrived at Azriel's side, and it raised the crown high. The queen mirrored the action.

King Augustus opened his mouth, and for the first time in years, his voice projected loudly over the audience.

"I hereby abdicate my throne and title as king of Arioch to my son, Azriel Faundor. For defeating the spawn of our great kingdom's symbols of power and privilege, he has earned this honor." A pause for silence, and then the queen placed the circlet on her husband's head. The king's crown rested atop Azriel's at the same time. It was lighter than he thought it would be, but the power in it filled him with elation.

"Long live Azriel Faundor, King of Arioch!"

Azriel was unsure who initiated the chant, but soon everyone was repeating the line over and over. He couldn't stop the grin stretching his mouth, dipping into his cheeks. He brightened, raising his arms triumphantly into the air.

They continued to cheer, even as Azriel turned around to face Viktor, whose expression was grave, his lips moving, the words silenced by whoops from the crowd.

But Azriel could read his mouth, the secret out. Immediately, the victory flushed from the new king's system, his stomach dropping and curdling with disbelief.

*Nadia has been found in Aldorin,* Viktor's lips formed to say. But they didn't stop there. Azriel swallowed a hard gulp of saliva as he processed the rushed words from his aide.

*And she has given birth to a son.*

# XI

# FATED

## Before the coronation of Azriel Faundor

Nadia and Bernadette traveled for several days after Viktor left them in Arcanvale, a human village bordering Aldorin. He'd dropped them off there per Nadia's request, though Bernadette had explained to her that they'd pretend to have left for Morath, across the Western sea. Bernadette was happy to comply with Nadia when she made her request to revisit her people.

When they finally crossed into the magical forest, Aldorin's domain seemed to awaken the dwindling magic within Nadia, making her elven features reemerge as if she *hadn't* been starved of magic for the past thousand years. She would soon discover that any and all of her attempts at using magic would fail, a reminder that her purpose had been lost.

The elf queen and lady spent several weeks wandering through the enchanted wood. Bernadette was too heavy to glide across the treetops as the elves did, so their progress was slow, marked by detours and long rests beneath the ancient boughs. Nadia intended for them to find her castle, Hearthstrom. She had already forgotten what it looked like, and wished to behold it again, to rekindle the memories she forfeited in Arioch's dungeons.

When they finally reached a small village south of Hearthstrom, there were only the remnants of the old building—nothing but broken stone and ivy.

The sight hollowed her.

She had imagined ruins, but not silence, not the way the land itself seemed to mourn. For a time, loss was all she felt. They remained in the small village for a week, allowing Nadia to feel the loss of what had long ago been hers. Doing so softened the dull ache she felt, and she realized with sadness that without a queen to guide them, her people would have no need for a castle. Maybe they had even grown to despise her... The thought brought her shame and a strange yet comforting revelation. A new chapter she could begin at last.

She decided to keep her name to herself, to let her people believe she was no one of importance. She made this choice before they continued on their journey, and Bernadette approved at once. It would serve both of them well to hide Nadia's true identity, and they agreed starting with her name was a wise decision.

To further conceal suspicions about their purpose for living in the forest, they made the quick decision to act as ambassadors from Morath. Elves weren't treated there in the same way they were in Arioch, so the pair spun a story the people of Aldorin would believe: she was a foreign elf sent by Morathan royalty to study the state of Arioch's enchanted wood, and Bernadette was her chaperone (despite Nadia's malnourishment, she still looked rather youthful). Karmin had gifted Bernadette the royal wax seal of Morath, and displaying it was all it took to make their tale credible. The princess deserved high praises if Nadia ever met her again.

Bernadette and Nadia settled in a small village in the east called Maen, where Nadia assumed her new name—Aidan.

Bernadette thought it a fitting choice. Under that name, the elf queen slipped easily into Aldorin life.

Her people were worse off than she predicted. They lived centuries with the honesty curse she cast upon them, so trust was fragile, even among friends and family. Though Maen was mostly kin, and they certainly treated her as an outsider, they also allowed her to stay and observe. She was kind to them, to their children. In time, she was entrusted with the young while their parents went to hunt or gather.

She grew fond of Maen's people, and after a while, she no longer considered the possibility the prince would find her and drag her back to the castle.

As the years passed, Bernadette confessed she felt like she belonged with the elven people, despite small aspects of noble life she sometimes missed. The way Nadia's people expressed love was more magical than Bernadette had thought imaginable. Beyond the bond that bound some elves together as mates, Aldorin's holy blessing magically entwining them, elves were intrinsically protective and just. *Honesty might have cursed them*, Bernadette had said one afternoon, *but truth has always been in their nature.*

Occasionally, elven merchants would travel through their small village, offering foreign clothes, trinkets, and enchantments. Every full moon, the village would host a festival where all young eligible elven women would wear imported clothing to attract the eyes of potential partners. This tradition had been established after Nadia was imprisoned beneath the castle. She had once been the confidant for unmarried women, but she did not mourn this responsibility. Rather, she was fascinated by this change in culture.

On normal nights, Nadia sat among others around a large fire and listened to stories told by both children and adults. Each story was retold with variations, but there was exactly one that remained the same, no matter who performed it.

It was the history of the War of Undying.

The first time it was told, Nadia nearly choked on the berries she'd shoveled into her mouth. The history was twisted, blaming the loss of the war on the fairies. The story was told with such malice, Nadia feared any attempts at correcting their erroneous beliefs would ruin all the trust she'd spent years building with them. How could she defend the fairies, whom they loathed so intensely? Whom, she later learned, they *still* fought with, tooth for tooth?

The story had been told incorrectly for many years, perverted with hate and vengeance for their lost queen, who happened to sit at the fire with them and listen to each rendition of the misconstrued history. Their queen, who would never admit her true identity to them.

Gradually, Nadia grew numb to the nighttime stories. They were fabricated, fiction. She told herself this, and it made things easier. This new false truth blurred her own past, helped her move on. She might have even believed the lies, if a little bit. The children were so adamant they were true...

Nadia had only just tasted the renewal she longed for when the dreams descended, fracturing her newfound peace.

They were of Azriel and his roaming hands. Of the night she spent with Karmin in the library, whispering the prophecy over parchment. The prophecy rang in her head each night, and she found it harder and harder to stay asleep. It was like Aldorin was warning her of the future that would soon come to pass.

Nadia made wandering to the stream behind Maen a nightly

occurrence, and eventually Bernadette followed her for company. The lady remained silent whenever Nadia splashed her face with the cold water, hoping the shock would shake the visions from her memory. Bernadette never asked what ailed Nadia, knowing that if the elf queen wished for it, she would tell her eventually.

But whether Nadia wanted to tell her friend or not, the prophecy's curse forbade her from speaking of it—or rather, the fear of losing her voice forever settled her decision to remain silent for her.

She would not have a child with Azriel. No, she *could* not. She was an elf and he, a human. Their involvement itself was taboo, and would damn her child to a life of judgment and misery. If the prophecy came to pass, it would only curse his life further. Whenever she imagined bearing the responsibility of such a terrible fate, she felt unwell.

So she turned to Bernadette on one of those nights, her hand holding her long black hair out of the way as she splashed her face with water, and she confessed, "I am old, my friend. But not so old that it is impossible for me to bear a child."

Bernadette seemed puzzled, but she nodded as though she understood and said, "You would make a splendid mother, I think."

Nadia smiled, but despair filled her. "How can I avoid destiny's cruel hand? Must I remain tied to the prince, even now?"

Bernadette may not have known the details of the prophecy, but in their time together, Nadia had finally confessed everything that happened between her and the crown prince. Bernadette had deeply empathized with Nadia then.

"If you have interest, you might consider taking a lover, Aidan." Bernadette spoke softly, but she had to be careful of any listening ears. "Put aside your worries and build a family. You may be older than I am, but your body has not aged, and your health is stronger than it ever has been. There is no better time than now."

"Time," Nadia echoed. Her years had been long indeed, and she had never imagined herself bearing children or losing her heart to another. The thought had simply never taken root. The possibility had never existed for her within her dark cell. But then Nadia remembered something, a passing remark from a villager in Maen. "There is a festival tonight." Her voice lifted. "Isn't there?"

Bernadette's smile was encouraging. "Yes, miss. Do you wish to join the eligible women?"

Nadia stared into the stream. Above it, the moon was full and resplendent—elven festivals always took place on the night when the moon was its brightest. It gave the water an appearance of pure silver.

The elf queen had little left to lose. She inclined her head in silent assent.

Bernadette sighed softly. "Come, then. Let us see you properly adorned. The festivities will soon be upon us."

For the first time since the night she fled the castle, Nadia wore rouge on her lips and dark kohl under her eyes. Her hair was braided and pinned behind her with the stems of gold leaves, lent to her by their village's matchmaker. She wore an off-the-shoulder robe that hugged her waist and cascaded to her ankles. On one side, the fabric was slit to her knee, offering her more mobility. Her pale skin was lighter than the whiteness of the dress, her legs like shooting stars occasionally peeking through the gap as she walked. Her feet were bare and freshly washed.

She joined a group of gathered elven women, all quite young, no older than twenty. Nadia's own youthful features let her blend among them without question. They all knew her by now, and none had ever sought to ask how old she truly was.

These young ladies were sweet, and giddy with excitement. Nadia knew each of them well, and for most, this night marked their first appearance at the festival as eligible brides.

"Aidan! At last!" Yuna, a brown-haired woman, gasped. "You look devastatingly beautiful!"

The others nodded enthusiastically. Nadia's cheeks heated and she inclined her head in thanks.

"I heard some of the men are visiting from Myrlbourne today. All eligible young women have been spoken for," another of the women giggled. Mylie. She had darker skin, a rarity among the elves. Her hair was coiled and dark, framing her heart-shaped face.

The girls clapped their hands giddily.

"As much as I care for the young men of *our* village, I do hope to find my match among a fresh set of faces!" Yuna winked at Nadia.

While she spoke, the familiar rhythm of the festival drums rang cacophonously into the night, marking the location of the festival.

It wasn't long before elves from neighboring villages drifted into the fray, shaking their hips and raising their hands in time with the jubilant music. Merchants arranged themselves around the stone braziers, their stalls rich with food and wares. The space thickened with warmth and voices, lively and bright with laughter. Even the canopies above seemed to shake and shiver with the night.

Each of the women was gifted a sheer, brightly colored sash, which they tied loosely about their heads, veiling their noses and mouths. Beyond the allure of mystery and soft seduction, the sashes marked them as the evening's prospective brides. Gill, the lively matchmaker with silver threading through her hair, offered each young woman an encouraging pat on the shoulder before sending them into the throng of bodies.

Nadia bumped into several people, none of whom paid her any mind. Laughter bubbled around her, excitement charged in the air.

For the first time in centuries, she was nervous. Would she find her match, or would her sash remain tied at the base of her skull? She knew some women ended the night without a partner, and the chances of her finding someone so easily were slim, but she dared to hope.

Her heart hammered against her ribs, and her body grew hot. The fires were away at the edges of the village's center, and yet, she felt as though one was right next to her, sending feverish mats of sweat to her neck.

*I can't do this. I can't risk it. It's...too selfish.*

Nadia still felt the weight of her sins, the wrongs she'd committed still in need of atonement.

She twirled, rising on her toes to weave through the press, only to collide with a solid, unyielding frame. She was pinned against a tall, thin man whose hair fell in a pale, thick rope over his shoulder.

He steadied her with firm hands. His ears were longer than she had seen in a while—they often represented pure-bloodedness or age, if not divinity. None of the elves she'd encountered in her recent travels bore her likeness as he did.

The ground cleared around them for a moment, and the music seemed to soften. The pounding in her heart overtook it, and soon it was all she could hear.

He captured her in his marble gaze of orange and green, a smile crooked on his lips. His lashes were light, wispy. Light hair was another rarity among elves—the purity of their magic usually appeared in their skin, which was pale and unblemished by the sun. But with this man, the color of Aldorin's magic bled into each strand of his long, soft hair.

"What is your name, maiden?" he asked.

"N—Aidan." Nadia caught herself, her throat bobbing.

"Nayden?"

"Aidan," she said. Her cheeks were scorching.

Memories rose to the surface then, roused by her quickening excitement. She had felt something similar with Azriel, but it had been years since, and she already convinced herself she was merely starved of touch. But this... This was different. Could she truly feel interest for a man she just met? She once laughed at the revelry of young romance, but perhaps, even for her, it was possible... She no longer felt inclined to cast the notion aside as she did before.

"What a fair name." He offered a dazzling smile that displayed his elegantly long canines, then pressed slender fingers to his chest and bowed low. "I am Lancenel. I come from Myrlbourne, yet I think you perceive more in me than my place of origin."

His eyes were now a charming sea foam green—the change a result of the curse she cast upon her people. Strangely, the familiar sting of guilt didn't show its face. Instead, she found herself caught in the tides of his warm gaze. Entranced.

"Indeed." Nadia swallowed. A thin, clammy warmth clung to her skin. Perhaps it was the heat of the dancing crowd, or maybe it was the great flames that roared around the festival's center...

*Neither*, a voice rang in her head.

She looked at Lancenel. He cocked his head at her, the smile still hanging on his lips as if it would be too bothersome for him to stop.

"We are both old souls, you and I." He extended his hand, open and waiting. She set her own in his, and they slipped into the current of moving bodies. Their steps aligned with quiet ease, movement answering movement. They did not drift too near, and

Nadia found herself glad for the distance. Lancenel simply watched her with quiet contentment, expecting nothing from her in return.

After two dances, Nadia gathered her courage, though her voice quivered. "You may lift my sash." Such permission was required, and granted only to a match an elven woman truly wished to consider.

Lancenel's eyes flashed, his Adam's apple jumping. He stilled, then reached forward carefully, untying the loose knot at the back of her head. The sash billowed into his hands.

His lips lifted. "Truly beautiful."

Nadia flushed. The heat surrounding her head was inescapable. "A-and yours, if you approve."

She felt distantly guilty about using this opportunity to combat the prophecy of her future child, but she was also genuinely attracted to the man studying her. Something about him called to her.

"Yes." The word was a breath that he inhaled as he drew her gently into his arms. "You may think me strange, but it feels as though this match has long been waiting for us. As though you and I were meant to cross paths...long ago."

The moment the words were spoken, Nadia's heart felt lighter, and she realized she felt the same way. Perhaps if she'd escaped much earlier, they might have met, and...

Nadia pushed away from him, gasping. The elves around them startled, but only momentarily. They returned to their swirling movements while her forearm had begun to burn with a sudden heat, painful and sharp. She clenched it and a moan rumbled in her throat. Lancenel winced next to her, something apparently afflicting him as well—but he wasn't looking at her. No, he was gripping his *own* arm. In the *same exact* location.

Nadia willed the pain away, able to barely heal herself. But her healing only removed the initial sting of pain—in its wake, a glowing spiral-shaped mark traveled up her arm and came to a point on her elbow.

Lancenel buckled, sucking in a breath as he clutched his arm, nails digging into flesh. His face contorted, his lips twisting.

But Nadia smiled, her hand flying to her mouth. Tears slipped from her eyes. She knew exactly what this meant. The low rumble of heat in her arm was sign enough. The familiarity she felt with Lancenel was no coincidence—their union had been ordained by none other than her heavenly mother, Aldorin.

They were blessed by the goddess, now a mated pair.

For all those years she was alone, Aldorin hadn't abandoned her.

Their marriage ceremony was a small thing—both of them preferred tender privacy.

Nadia discovered that though she was older than Lancenel, he also bore regal blood, which slowed the timeline of his long life. He was nearly two hundred years old, whereas most elves lived to one hundred, if they were in good health.

On their wedding day, Nadia wore white lilies in her hair and a simple leaf-sewn gown with woven wheatgrass stitching that, when dried, glimmered like gold thread. Her audience consisted of the few young women who had been with her on the night she met Lancenel, along with an elder sage who spoke blessings over them in the name of Aldorin.

In that moment, Nadia feared she could never deserve the happiness this ceremony symbolized. She had lived so long, trapped in darkness, and her heavenly mother hadn't intervened once. But the blessing, the bond between her and Lancenel, was a

clear sign from Aldorin—their union was meant to be, and every trial before this moment had been the path fate required of her.

She was so, so...*happy*.

Nadia cupped her hands under her chin and watched as the children laughed and played outside her straw-and-clay hut. Lancenel slumbered on the bed behind her, his too-long legs extending far past the end of the grass-filled mattress.

The breeze lifted the elf queen's dark hair from her shoulders. She breathed in the scent—pine and salt.

At last, she had found peace.

She was beginning to allow herself to love this new life. It had been nearly five years since she fled, and not once did she see a soldier or hear of the prince searching for her. She imagined Karmin kept him busy, and though she never planned on seeing the princess again, she occasionally sent prayers to Aldorin for her protection.

Bernadette's knock on their thin reed door was quiet, but Nadia had expected her to come, so she was listening for it. Elves had heightened hearing and sight compared to all other creatures, so Bernadette was forced to adopt different habits. Her specific rasping knock was used when she didn't want Lancenel to hear. She wanted to speak with Nadia—alone.

Tucking her hair behind her, Nadia padded gently across the clay ground and brushed past the door, careful not to disturb her husband.

Bernadette clasped Nadia's hands, running her thumbs gingerly over the elf's small knuckles.

The lady had a glow about her that hadn't been there during their time at the castle. Bernadette had grown much more relaxed, a smile on her face at all times. Nadia wondered if Maen was where the lady truly belonged, and if more humans like her existed.

Bernadette's eyes flitted to Nadia's waist. She rested her hand above Nadia's navel. Her thumb stroked it softly, the roundness beginning to show through Nadia's tunic and braies. She had purposefully been wearing Lancenel's—with slight alterations—so others wouldn't suspect her. But Bernadette saw through it all, and checked on Nadia frequently to see if she would be able to carry a child through to term.

"He's growing larger." Her smile was brighter than the early morning sun. "He's healthy."

Nadia rested her hand over Bernadette's, which was still massaging circles over her stomach. "You seem convinced the baby is a boy."

Occasionally, Bernadette's face would ease into that serene, eternal countenance, the edges of her features dissolving. In those moments, even Nadia—with centuries of life etched into her own being—perceived Bernadette, rather than herself, as the all-knowing immortal whose guidance must be followed.

The lady wore such an expression now.

*How strange*, Nadia thought, *that a human can carry such divinity.*

Whenever Bernadette's face seemed not her own, it lasted for only a moment before her features would wrinkle once more, and the lady would return to coddling her.

"It must be a feeling only a woman who has never had children of her own can experience," she said. Her voice was brittle, but Nadia assumed this was because the lady was trying to stay quiet. Bernadette shook her head, a wild smile stretching into her cheeks. "It is time to visit the physician. I mean, the *healer*."

Nadia nodded, and a strange knot formed in her throat. Her palms grew clammy, and her knees trembled. What if the healer gave her bad news?

Bernadette didn't sense Nadia's stress as she led her across the village discreetly to the healer's hut. Malry was likely still asleep after a long week of healing the cuts and bruises of rambunctious elven children. This would be Nadia's first visit for health issues not related to her appetite and eating habits.

Before they entered Malry's home, Bernadette turned to Nadia and squeezed her hand. "Good news will come of this, miss. You will soon be able to share this knowledge with your beloved. Oh, how happy he will be!"

Nadia swallowed a nervous breath and nodded. Her quaking lips couldn't quite pull into a smile.

Bernadette pulled them through the entrance and into the large, dark space.

Malry shifted in sleep, moaning something about tinctures. Then she shot up, her golden brown hair a mess. Her eyes searched the room with alertness, and when they stopped on the two intruders, she relaxed.

"I thought yiz were them damn klopses again," the healer swore, leaping from her cot and pulling on a thin robe to cover herself. She knotted the ends of a string together after twisting it about her middle. "No matter. What can I do yiz for?"

Bernadette clapped her hands. "Feel for yourself, Malry. We are in need of your expert appraisal."

"Expert heh?" Malry was enthused by the unintended compliment.

She reached toward Nadia, pressing small hands gently to her belly. After a few seconds, she nodded.

"Can ya sit up here?" The healer pointed to an elevated table surrounded by containers filled with salves, tinctures, and simple vials of witch potions. Nadia noticed the dried flowers hanging from twine pinned to the wall—roses and peonies. They would need them for the celebration of her child's birth.

Bernadette helped Nadia atop the table and gently laid her back. Nadia winced at the cold of the wood.

Malry climbed onto a stool so she could assess Nadia from a higher point, then set her tools to the side. She informed Nadia each time before she attempted to touch her, and spoke aloud whenever she discovered something.

A smile lifted the pale healer's lips. "A healthy one." Her hands shifted on Nadia's stomach. "Heartbeat's steady. He's about halfway grown."

Nadia's heart leapt at the use of "he." If she was having a boy, she would have successfully defeated the prophecy. Her womb would bear an *elven* son, one who would live a normal life, tucked away from wicked kings and heirs. She desperately hoped the healer wasn't merely using the common pronoun.

Malry turned and dragged her finger across a saucer of red paste. She gently touched Nadia's upper abdomen, right below the ribs. She drew a line with the paste, then pulled Nadia's tunic back over her belly.

"This can track yer baby's growth. Best to watch fer movement. He'll start kickin' y'all over. Won't feel too great. But it's a good sign. This yer first?"

The elf queen nodded. Butterflies filled her stomach, and she remembered the last time she'd felt this way—when she'd first met Lancenel. Her thoughts no longer lingered on Azriel and the worry that once plagued her. She accepted this peace. Her new chapter was finally beginning.

"Ya have my congratulations," Malry said. She hopped from the table and dropped her supplies in a wash basin. She didn't look at Nadia as she muttered, "And dare I say, good luck."

# XII
# FOUND

Azriel made preparations immediately.

Exactly one day after he was crowned king, Azriel called the visiting nobility and selected his council from among them. Their first meeting was quick—he informed them of his decision to venture out in search of his long-lost consort. Several of this new council were his father's men, who greatly disapproved of his decision.

"You *just* ascended the throne, Your Majesty. There are duties you must attend to here." One of the nobles rushed to speak, the graying hairs atop his head few and frazzled. "It is unreasonable to leave for a mere consort when our kingdom is in such a state."

All Azriel heard was defiance. The anger boiling in his blood cooled him.

He didn't have to think twice before he raised a hand, and one of his personal soldiers ran the noble through with a longsword. The man toppled from his chair, his eyes glossy and angled at the crimson hole in his chest.

The rest of the council said nothing, their faces tight with fear and conflicted loyalty.

"I will depart today," Azriel growled. "Our kingdom is not in any current state of duress, but if you must contact me whilst I am gone, send for a mage." The king leveled his gaze at the group of men in his court, who nodded unanimously.

Without another word, Azriel stormed from the room.

Viktor followed him into the corridor. Six soldiers silently fell into step behind them.

"Have you your communication rune, Your Majesty?"

Azriel grunted his response. He didn't wish to speak to anyone. His thoughts warred in his head, a flurry of rage, desire, and regret, not for killing the noble, but for telling them of his plans at all. His council's job was to help him make decisions, and his mind was already made.

They arrived at the royal stables. Servants had already prepared armored warhorses for them—dressed in metallic plating and armor for their heads, the horses stood obediently in a line.

Azriel approached the stallion bearing the flag of Arioch. He flung a leg over the beast and gripped the reins in one hand. He hadn't bothered to dress in anything more than a tunic and chain mail, because he did not foresee having to fight anyone on this journey. The crown atop his head and the presence of warhorses would intimidate any onlookers.

With a whistle, Azriel commanded his entourage to leave the castle grounds. They obediently followed him into Bellmane, the bustling castletown.

They paid little attention to the cowering peasants who fell to their knees at the sight of him, nor to the merchants who froze with their wares, shock slackening their jaws as the group passed through the town.

As king, Azriel would do as he pleased. Usually, the spilling of blood sated the fire in his chest—but this time, his limbs trembled with anger of a peculiar sort.

Nadia had a son? And who... By *whom*?

He decided it didn't matter. He would easily get rid of the man who impregnated his woman, and he would slaughter the son, too. Nadia would see reason, she *had* to. She *belonged* to him, owed her *life* to him. If he hadn't taken her out of that cold, dark dungeon, she would still be there. Rotting away.

And *this* was how she thanked him?

His heart ached. He still couldn't believe Nadia had left of her own accord. Even the damned Lady Bernadette disappeared. After years of her accompaniment, she was the last person he suspected to betray him so cruelly.

The soldiers remained silent behind him, but Viktor cleared his throat at his side.

"Speak if you have something to say, Vik. Did my demonstration in the war room fail to cow you?"

The fairy duke laughed airily, and Azriel could almost taste the visceral fear in it. He found the sound of it rather...soothing. He much preferred it to the uncertain ground around their camaraderie. Friendship was impossible between them, and any illusion of it weakened his authority.

"I may know where to learn of Nadia's whereabouts." Viktor's jaw tensed as he measured his words. "But first, I must ask, Your Majesty, if I might be so bold..."

Azriel raised a brow. "Go on."

Viktor lowered his voice. "What do you intend for the elf, Your Majesty? She has committed treason. Would it not be fitting to offer her to your great ancestor?"

Azriel's knuckles turned white around the reins. His frown deepened.

In truth, he hadn't planned what to do with Nadia once he found her. Had he come to loathe her so much that he would *kill* her?

His heart pinched with pain, giving him his answer.

"No," was all he said.

They traveled for many hours, passing through small towns

until they reached the very edge of Arioch's human dominion—Arcanvale, the bustling town filled with trade between the enchanted forest and the human kingdom. Azriel had passed through a few times when he fought wars on the eastern border. He often had to travel through the forest itself to reach the eastern coast. The forest interested him little, yet now, as his eyes fell upon the dark trees framing Arcanvale's bustling heart, a hot, sudden fury seized him.

Somewhere inside, Nadia was cradling a child in her arms, nursing him with love.

It was not *his* child.

Azriel breathed deeply, cracked his neck, then turned on his soldiers.

"Break here for an hour. After you've satisfied your hunger, we will proceed into Aldorin." He surveyed the group, his eyes sharp. "No ale. Fill your flasks with water and break bread at the town's tavern, then meet me back here."

The soldiers nodded once, heads bobbing in sync. They dismounted their horses and tied the reins to posts outside the town's center before scattering. Viktor stayed with Azriel as he dropped from his horse and secured it to a post.

"Your Majesty, look." Viktor's finger pointed discreetly from his waist, aiming at the town square.

Azriel followed to where his aide directed. A group of haggard, gray-haired women sat crouched around a rusted cauldron. An impressive steam billowed above a boiling concoction within. The women wailed, though their squeals were suppressed slightly by the crowd bubbling around them.

"We've seen witches before," Azriel said. "Crazy wenches."

"No, *look*," Viktor pressed. Azriel glared at his aide in warning, but the fairy duke was too distracted by the gaggle of women praising their cauldron to notice. "They're beckoning you. I can smell the scent of Faundor blood from here—I'm curious where they obtained it... They flaunt it in wait for a member of your bloodline to grant them an audience."

Azriel watched the women warily. Their eyes were clouded over, unseeing. Witches weren't magical beings—they were humans with an inclination for practicing evil deeds and predicting futures of the damned. He'd never spoken to one before, for as a child he feared his own future would be cursed. They didn't often appear before him, so he had long forgotten their existence. A small part of him still bristled at Viktor's observations.

"What good will come from speaking with them?" Azriel asked. "Let them wait for a different Faundor child. They will entertain no audience from me."

The witches continued to wail after him, but the king stomped around them to the tavern on the other side. He pushed the heavy door open.

His men were seated at a long table, muttering amongst themselves. Each held half a loaf of rye bread in one hand and a pint of milk in the other.

Azriel approached the tavern's counter and ordered himself a bowl of hearty squash soup in addition to the other rations. The innkeeper prepared the milk, bread and soup, but his face had gone pale, his voice dry as he confirmed the king's order.

Azriel took his food and sat among his men, who quieted at his presence. They continued their meal in silence. Around them, patrons did not dare to speak. The innkeeper sat behind the counter, biting his fingernails.

Once they finished, they left the tavern with a gloom over their heads. The soldiers mumbled amongst themselves again as they distanced themselves from the king.

Azriel paused to survey the town, which was still busy with merchants and customers chittering about. But the witches—and their bubbling cauldron—were gone.

Aldorin was beautiful, but Azriel hated it.

Long ago, when Arioch Faundor won the War of the Undying, he sought to seize the forest as well. Some unseen force thwarted him, and he died shortly after his son, Benjamin—the youngest king of Arioch—had turned ten.

Azriel did not place his faith in elven gods and goddesses, yet he could not entirely dismiss the feeling that some power acted of its own will. Perhaps even the forest itself. When Azriel and his men entered the enchanted wood, he expected vines to reach around their horses' legs and tug them into the earth to bury them alive. He imagined the rage of the forest, of Aldorin's wrath at the ancient altercation between his ancestors and the magical beasts the forest protected. He pictured himself as the forest's target, entering its grounds willingly, like a fool.

But despite the doom he felt, nothing happened. Rather, creatures scurried around them, creating a path for them. Winged creatures with hideous faces, gnarly bark-skinned creatures with large soulless eyes, and purple-skinned creatures with bone-thin frames walked along the edges of the road, displeasure bleeding off them as easily as sweat.

He did his best to pay them no mind. Azriel knew very little about magic, but it was enough to understand the paradox by which it was bound: all magic sprang from a pure source, and no matter the wielder's intent, it could not be twisted toward harm or evil. It could not take life, lay curses, or be forged into weapons. So, though scornful, the creatures' stares would not harm him.

Only the mages—humans transformed by magic—could

pervert the original intent of magic. They were one of the many reasons Arioch had succeeded in the ancient war.

Azriel preferred to leave the court mages to their own bidding within the castle, and did not like bringing them along with him as his father and grandfather did. He preferred the less obvious, reliable loyalty of his oath-bound fairy aide.

It was dusk when they arrived at their first elven village after hours of prodding along an unpaved path. The soldiers dismounted and passed their reins to a few cowering children, who looked as though they were seeing horses for the first time in their lives.

Azriel was bemused by their uncertainty.

Four soldiers stayed with their horses and entertained brief conversations with the children, who didn't seem to understand the Ariochan tongue.

Viktor and the two remaining soldiers followed Azriel into the village. The houses were round and small, made of mud and sticks. A small communal fire pit sat in the center, with dirty cushions placed around it. Villagers clutched one another in their doorways, eyes wide.

Azriel made eye contact with each of them, noting how their eyes flickered to black. "I am looking for an elven woman." His voice echoed off the surrounding trees. Mothers and daughters retreated quickly into their homes and the men stepped forward, eyes hard.

Azriel imagined Nadia in one of these homes, hugging her babe in the dark of her own hut while her husband stepped forward to protect her from him.

A vicious smile spread over the king's lips.

"Her name is Nadia, and if she is here, I must take her with me."

Seconds passed, and the men's faces went from defensive to relieved.

In broken Ariochan tongue, one of the men stepped forward and said, "Nadia is, here, not."

"Viktor," the king said. His aide thudded a fist over his chest, heeding his king's command. "You speak their language. Tell them what will happen if they hide her from me."

Viktor cleared his throat. "And what would you have me say, Your Majesty?"

Azriel barked a laugh. His lips flattened to a cruel line. "Be creative."

Viktor nodded gravely. The man who spoke wore no shoes and scraggly clothes, but his body was tethered with muscle. His hands were fisted at his sides, ready to defend his family.

Viktor spoke the language of the elves, but Azriel couldn't tell what it was he said. The reactions of the villagers, though, told him his aide had indeed been creative with his words. Color drained from their already-pale faces.

The elf offered a hurried plea in his native tongue, his voice trembling. He placed a shaky hand over his chest and knelt, pressing his forehead into the dirt.

"He said if they hear anything about an elven woman with dark hair who goes by Nadia, they will report her to their leaders and send her to you." Viktor puffed his chest proudly. "But it really does appear she is not in this village. Shall we move on to the next?"

Azriel huffed and eyed the villagers, who bent their heads to him.

They left without another word.

Azriel and his soldiers continued east. They spent three nights at unassuming taverns, two of which were miles apart but went by the same name—Pally's on the Bend. Each night spent at these taverns was strange, for the owner was the same odd piggish woman, stout with gold tinted skin and dragonlike scales that shimmered all over her body. Azriel couldn't fathom how two of the same taverns could exist with the same owner, and at first he didn't try to understand it. But when they arrived at the second Pally's, the owner remembered them and snarled as she handed them their room keys.

Azriel could have killed her, but he didn't see the point. All of the residents of Aldorin reacted similarly to him—her distaste was simply more personal. Viktor reminded him of his mission. This ugly woman wasn't directly defying him as his councilman had, and she posed no threat to him, even with her clawed fingers.

When she hissed at him, cursing him to never return, he merely smiled.

He stayed an extra night to spite her.

After a little more than a week, they traveled more than half of Aldorin, visiting at least fifteen elven villages. Nadia was in none of them. To fight the exhaustion weighing him down, Azriel made sure to check the faces of each villager. It forced him to remain alert. They trembled in his presence, but he discovered none of them housed his runaway lover. If Arioch's history books were accurate, elves were incapable of telling lies, so he had no reason to not believe them.

During their travels to one of these villages, a messenger from the castle intercepted them, informing Azriel of his father's condition. Apparently, when Augustus heard of Azriel's expedition to Aldorin, his health had declined severely, and hadn't moved from his bed in a week. This news, along with Azriel's ongoing directionless search, gnawed away at the fury in his chest.

He realized he was losing what drove him to find her, and

when he tried to reinvigorate himself with the image of Nadia's new lover clinging to her, instead he felt an empty, hopeless tug of anger that dropped to his stomach.

The next village they stopped at was smaller than most of the ones they'd visited, so Azriel didn't have much hope Nadia would be there. He suspected she would want to hide among crowds, not to be easily spotted among members of a small community.

His soldiers were tired too. He was ready to be finished with his search, and he imagined they were moreso. It wasn't mercy, but exhaustion that led him to order his soldiers to stay behind at a day tavern to eat while he and Viktor entered the village on foot. It was close enough that untying their horses seemed unnecessary.

Viktor gulped water as they walked, smeared the wetness from his lips with the back of his hand, then stretched his arms. "Do you think we will find her here? Or perhaps my sources were wrong, and she's truly fled the continent as we originally suspected?"

Azriel considered the possibility. "If you *are* wrong, you will be who I punish for sending me on this pointless journey."

Viktor blanched, clearing his throat. "Yes, Your Majesty. Let us hope she is here. I am not sure where else she would be."

They stepped into the village, bodies slouched. Village children danced around an unlit fire pit and a few women were hanging clothes to dry on lines between the trees shrouding their small community. Most of the kids had dark-colored hair, brown like soot or red like autumn leaves. But one had bright yellow hair, almost gold when the sun shone upon it. He looked to be the youngest, wobbling around on chunky legs.

A tall, lanky elf with similarly-colored hair scooped the child in his arms and nuzzled him with a nose, smiling so warmly it hurt the king to watch.

He turned away, opening his mouth to order Viktor away, for

he knew they were both tired and ready to admit defeat. He had been thorough in his search, and he could not reason why Nadia would settle in a village as remote as this one. Though he was loath to admit it, his council had been right. He needed to return and begin his reign as their new king. He was wasting time. Frolicking like a lovesick bird.

Before Azriel's words left his lips, a sound rang throughout the village with a familiar timbre... one that made him freeze. He could not move, could not turn to see what had made the sound.

It was the laughter of the heavens—so beautiful, it struck him into silence. So exquisite, it first lifted him with elation, only for that joy to be scorched away by a heat of outrage that raked through him to his core.

The child giggled in response, and its mother's voice carried like a melody across the village. Its note strummed the chords of Azriel's heart, seizing him with longing he hadn't felt in years.

"Your Majesty?" Viktor looked at the king, clearly not aware they found her. They *found* Nadia. No, instead the aide focused on the king's frozen, clenched fists.

When Azriel finally turned around, the village had gone silent. He stared directly into Nadia's eyes. They were a bright hazel that held a bundle of emotions he couldn't decipher. She was frightened, but her expression betrayed more than simple fear. The elf man next to her slipped his arm around her waist, concern etched into his features.

"Nadia." Azriel's voice was pained, and, damn him, he could not hide the emotion in it. Surprise flashed across her face, and she looked quickly to Viktor. Her eyebrows pinched together.

It was then Azriel noticed the child had disappeared.

Anger restored itself anew.

"I found you."

Nadia gulped and closed her eyes. Her lips trembled. Tears slid unbidden down her cheeks.

"Your Majesty," the blond elf said. His words were clear, spoken in perfect Ariochan. Azriel glared at him, his hands flexing at his sides. "I am not sure who you are looking for, but certainly it is not my wife, Aidan?"

Azriel worked his jaw. "*Aidan*?"

Viktor leaned toward the king. "Nadia, spelled in reverse?"

Azriel barked a laugh, then twisted his face into a scowl.

"Kill him." The order was clear, final. It was blood-binding—Viktor had no choice but to obey. But Azriel felt good in command. He knew he wouldn't regret this decision.

Azriel watched the fear swirl in his aide's eyes, even as the duke rigidly plucked his sword from its sheath and advanced on the tall elf.

Nadia's lover separated himself from her, pushing her aside with such force, she fell to the ground and winced. The rest of the small community shuttered themselves behind reed doors, helplessly witnessing the altercation.

A ball of flame pooled within the man's palm, and he spread it into a long rod shape. He held it like a weapon, but it did nothing against the solid metal blade Viktor drove through his chest. The fairy was quick, pushing the blade deeper until carmine liquid leaked from the wound and stained the front of the man in a burst. The duke twisted the blade, a demented darkness in the black of his eyes, in the tick of his lips as they pulled into an inhuman grin that mirrored Azriel's intent.

The elf man shrieked, his face contorting, his lips shaking. His eyes flicked desperately to Nadia, who clutched her own chest, shrieking in pain as if her husband's pain was her own.

"No!" Nadia clawed at the ground. "Lancenel, *no*!"

Her voice carried such dread, such intense emotion, it made Azriel's anger curdle into something even greater—loathing. A deep, immediate hatred for what Nadia had done, for the love she afforded this man but had not given to him, the *king*. He had offered her everything, and she rejected it to live a life in a shabby hut with a man who had *nothing*.

"Viktor, enough. He is dead." Azriel's voice was ice. The duke had stabbed the elf man twice more, the glint in his eyes wicked, drunk on the bloodshed. The elf man—Lancenel—had no life left in his eyes, his body hunched in on itself, limp.

Viktor slid his bloody sword back into its sheath, then he kicked the body over. It thudded softly against the dirt.

Nadia continued to cry, banging her hand against her chest. Her face was stained with never-ending tears. Her mouth shook as she sobbed, the sound of her misery crashing around them.

"Take her," Azriel said. Viktor snickered, the look on his face filled with unbridled pleasure at obeying his sovereign's order.

The duke wrenched the elf off the ground and slung her over his shoulder. She continued to cry, her arms weakly hitting Viktor's shoulder.

They left the village. No one dared to stop them. Nadia continued to thrash against Viktor, but the fairy duke held her tightly.

When they returned to the tavern, Azriel ordered Viktor to bind her hands together with rope and tie a damp cloth around her head and mouth.

The king and his men departed in silence. The soldiers seemed relieved to have finally found the woman. They even spoke loudly about the success of their king, boasting his honor.

Azriel's thoughts were far from the child he had orphaned, spirited away somewhere safe amidst the chaos. The child would never know his mother, nor his father. The babe couldn't have been much older than a year. Azriel didn't take joy in slaying children, but he also had to force himself not to worry about the one he let live. He killed the man who had stolen Nadia's heart, and that would have to suffice.

THE RIDE to his castle was long and quiet. Nadia grew sadder each day, her lips colorless after being held open for days with the cloth. Her eyes were red-rimmed from crying—she often wept at night, in her sleep. Azriel and his men could hear her, even though he gave her a separate guarded room at each of the taverns where they rested.

Before they entered Bellmane, tired from their journey but spirited enough to have the energy to celebrate the conclusion of their mission, Azriel's stomach tightened.

He let the baby live—his first blunder—but he also failed to find Nadia's accomplice, Bernadette. Could her disappearance have been unrelated to Nadia after all? Maybe Bernadette, who had served him since he was a young boy, hadn't truly betrayed him.

Azriel turned to his soldiers. Two of them appeared significantly more energized than the others. He pointed at them.

"I failed to retrieve a human noblewoman, Lady Bernadette Ferle. Return to the eastern village and within the week, bring the lady to the castle. If you do not find her there, you may return empty-handed. If you *do* find her, bring her to me alive." He waved the soldiers off. Their expressions revealed nothing, but the subtle sag of their shoulders as they walked away betrayed the weight of their disappointment.

"The rest of you," he said to Viktor and the four remaining soldiers, "well done. Drink your fill of ale tonight and rest well."

Nadia glared up at him from the back of Viktor's horse.

Azriel smiled at her, but it lacked mirth. He was not happy—not in any ordinary sense. It was the cruel blend of revulsion he felt toward the elf and the grim satisfaction he anticipated in making her pay for her betrayal.

He wouldn't kill her, no. Because something else stirred in his heart. A certain unfulfilled pleasure he knew he had yet to experience.

A twisted form of love. A dominance, he realized, he had wanted all along.

He was nice to her before.

Now he would be egregiously hostile.

# XIII

# COMPANION

Nadia's hands clasped together so tightly, her pale fingers had gone purple. She bent her neck to the small bed in the chamber Azriel had thrown her in, her silent tears soiling the white coverlet. Her prayers were chaos, a jumble of curses and pleas to her heavenly mother.

It had already been four days since Azriel dragged her from her new home and deposited her in this empty room.

Four days since her husband's life was stolen right before her eyes.

Four days since her blessed mark started its slow, agonizing death.

Four days since she abandoned her precious son.

Her body ached, her skin a sheen of fragile ice that fractured over her broken heart.

"Why?" Her voice cracked out, barely a whisper. She trembled as she spoke. "Why did you take them from me? Why won't you leave me alone?"

Her agony wracked her body, sobs labored her breaths.

Tragedy stung her, raw. Her hiccups and sobs were so intense, she did not hear when the door finally re-opened and someone entered the room.

She did not stir when the mattress creaked, nor when a hand rested at the base of her neck.

"Nadia."

The elf queen flinched, then relaxed. She lifted her head, relieved it wasn't Azriel come to visit her at last.

Karmin wore a gold-threaded night gown. A silver circlet was woven into her chestnut hair. Her body was thinner, but she carried herself with strength and confidence. Nadia hardly recognized her. A thin silver ring rested on the fourth finger of her left hand, the diamond embedded in it winking in the evening light.

"I thought I told you not to return."

Emotion bit behind Nadia's eyes, and she turned to press her face to the bed once more. Karmin stroked Nadia's back slowly, comfortingly.

"I do not hate you," the queen continued. "I learned of what happened. Bernadette has been speaking with me via letters sent through the Sanvira. She is doing well, and said not to fuss over her."

Nadia felt only a little relieved at the news. Her heart was in desperate need of repair—it was unraveling like a spool of thread she knew was nearing its end.

Karmin continued, "I am so sorry for your loss. Bernadette told me your beloved was a kind man, caring and loving and entirely focused on protecting you and your child."

Silent tears continued to spill from Nadia's eyes.

Anger bloomed within her, making its first appearance since she was ripped from her peaceful dream.

She understood Karmin was attempting to comfort her, but the human queen could not understand what Nadia had gone through. Not because loss was exclusive to elves, for what greater similarity between their people could there be than grief, sorrow, and despair? No, Nadia simply could not accept her sympathy, because to elves, a mating bond tethered souls together. She had been magically blessed, bound to her husband.

The consequence of the severance was unbearable.

Nadia was but a husk. The soul who had warmed her, the redemption she experienced with her mate... It was gone. *He* was gone. Perhaps she took him for granted, latching on to the hope that she would never experience such painful loss after everything she went through.

She was beginning to learn such hope was a human machination, never meant for her to enjoy.

Though Nadia's heart was heavy and her voice near the point of shattering beyond repair, she whispered, "Does something ail you, Your Majesty?"

Karmin removed her hand from Nadia's back. With a moment of hesitation, she rested her bejeweled hand over her navel. She gave it two gentle pats, a bitter smile twitching on her lips.

"I am to have a baby soon," she said. "Whether it is a boy or a girl, I do not know yet. I came to tell you of the news." Karmin's hand dropped and her face went stony. "I also wanted to convey my deepest apologies for what happened to yours. I cannot imagine..."

Nadia stopped listening. Her head swirled with happy memories of her little family, but each of these memories darkened at the edges, already fading into the rest of her limitless eternity.

She didn't notice when Karmin left, because she had fallen asleep, tears wetting the covers beneath her. And she didn't wake, not even when large hands lifted her and slid the covers over her cold body.

Not even when cruel lips grazed her mouth, damning her to her new life as an adulteress.

Karmin returned the following morning. She wished to tell Nadia about the letter she received that morning, which revealed Bernadette's imminent return to the castle. Most of their letters were encoded, using words to convey meaning beyond the obvious. They had to take care, for every letter was checked by a guard or noble or the king himself. Even with this cautiousness, however, the queen knew the king was growing suspicious of Bernadette's whereabouts.

Karmin had told him Lady Ferle was attending court in Morath, chasing the faint promise of a noble match. But with each passing year, it became harder to persuade Azriel of Bernadette's unsurmountable optimism.

Nadia stirred. She was very quiet in sleep, so quiet Karmin thought she might have died in her sleep. When the elf queen finally awoke, her face was sunken, distressed. Her eyes were red-rimmed. She'd cried the day prior, when Karmin had visited, and she probably wept throughout the night.

Who was Karmin to bother a grieving mother and widow? She felt torn about visiting her, but her own sickness was finally showing its effects, softening her over the years. She found herself in desperate want of a friend, for she had none. Could she find such shameless companionship in the woman her husband had committed such terrible atrocities against?

Karmin was grateful she hadn't grown severely ill in the past few years, as her physicians told her she would. The sickness crept in small, persistent ways: stiffness in her limbs each morning, tremors in her hands that were difficult to hide, spells of fatigue that stole from her waking hours. She had grown weaker, yes, but her will was no less fierce. As she looked upon Nadia, her heart stirred with an unexpected tenderness. Nadia had grown healthier since their last meeting, but she still looked as though a sudden wind might scatter her into dust. Grief held her together more tightly than flesh did.

When Nadia saw Karmin at the foot of her bed, she flinched in surprise. Then, recognizing her, her eyes dulled—not with anger, but with exhaustion—and she sank back into her pillow.

"His Majesty departed for the Midran warfront at dawn. Tensions rise by the day, or so the council claims." The queen kept her voice light, almost careless, as though war were a distant nuisance. To her, political affairs were trifles when compared with the matters of the heart.

"The child is due when the leaves begin to turn," she continued gently. "If the nobles' mutterings hold any truth, the king may not return in time to see the birth."

Nadia slowly, shakily, lifted herself so she was sitting eye-level with the queen. Karmin realized Nadia probably wanted something—*anything*—to concentrate on to distract herself from the oppressive thoughts and memories plaguing her.

"Would you like to attend my child's birth?"

Karmin felt nervous making the offer, but the surprise in Nadia's face was a good sign.

Distractedly, Nadia shifted her gaze and gnawed on her lip. She pulled the bedcovers from her legs.

She was quite small, but elegant. Were she a human, she would be considered malnourished and depraved, but because she was an elf, she was radiant. Karmin might have envied her, were it not for the quiet knowledge that both of them were slowly, helplessly fading.

Nadia merely wore her decline more gracefully—her beauty was nothing more than a gentle lie which covered the same quiet ruin.

At last, Nadia nodded. "Yes, I think I would enjoy that."

Karmin beamed. "I also wished to inform you that Bernadette will be returning to us soon. I am relieved. I have missed her."

Nadia stared absently at the wall by the door.

Karmin clicked her tongue, then stood from the bed.

"I hold the castle in the king's absence," Karmin said. "But do not let me stop you from engorging on food and drink. Of course, you cannot run away. Not anymore. I fear what the king might do to me if I let you slip away the moment he brought you back."

When Nadia's eyes flashed to Karmin, it looked as if she wished to bite her.

"I would send you away in a heartbeat if I could, Nadia, I swear it. But I cannot. I am the king's wife. I have duties to uphold. Though I run the castle in his stead, I still must bow to his whims. He instructed me to be watchful of you." Karmin smiled as warmly as she could. She wetted her lips. "Would you join me for tea in the library? I so abhor the company of the court ladies. They seem to want nothing to do with an ill queen."

Karmin did not wait for Nadia to respond. She brushed her hands together and sighed. "I take tea at noon. If you find yourself inclined to, do join me. I've many questions about motherhood—and no shortage of complaints about marriage."

Karmin left the room, closing the doors softly behind her. The moment the latch clicked, a tightness coiled in her chest. Heat flooded her stomach. Her fingertips prickled, then went numb, the sensation moving toward her elbows. Her throat rasped, dry and raw.

And then she couldn't breathe.

Months passed in quiet, unremarkable succession. As Karmin had predicted, the king did not return.

Nadia never came to take tea with the queen. She wished to, but Karmin's illness struck the moment she left Nadia's chamber that day, choking the breath from her and stealing her strength for weeks. By the time Karmin could sit upright again, the physicians had made their decree: she would be watched, tended to, and kept in her bed. The palace moved softly around her, as if afraid to disturb what little life she still held onto.

In that same stretch of time, the mark on Nadia's arm was nearly completely faded, no longer fed by the forest's magic, no longer bound to another's life.

Privately, the elf queen held a funeral for her husband and child. She forced herself to believe they were dead... The alternative was too cruel to bear. The thought of her baby boy growing old without knowing his mother hollowed her. It comforted her, however faintly, to think of him at peace beside his father rather than lost in a world she could no longer reach.

When she wasn't convincing herself she would escape her nightmare soon, she sat in her old spot in the library, back curved against the rounded window. She was still unable to read Ariochan script, so she stared instead at the garden and wrote her worries and anxieties into the foggy condensation her breath made on the glass. Usually these appeared as one-word epiphanies, but sometimes, when she felt she had a little more energy, she wrote lyrical poetry, legends, or histories long-forgotten.

Nadia felt helpless. She knew histories were being rewritten, misconstrued. But she was unable to stop it. It was not her duty, not her purpose to end the perversion of prophecy. She understood, painfully, that humans had grown to despise her people. Viktor hadn't given her the elixirs, so her identity was no longer concealed to the castle's servants. She grew into the habit of covering her ears and she rarely spoke to anyone. She made it her goal to become as interesting as the dirt-filled cracks in the stone floor—maybe once she achieved such a feat, the king wouldn't notice her when he eventually returned from battle.

As the days ticked by, Nadia's resentment grew for him. It was at its most intense when he had freshly stolen her from her village and killed her beloved, but time away from the king felt surreal, as if he had never done those things. Not seeing him roaming the castle halls made it horrifically easy to forget.

The many years of Nadia's life often squished together, crowded, too many. But she could clearly remember the days of joy she experienced with Lancenel and her son. They were the lights of her life. When she thought of them this way, she realized the continuation of the darkness of her past felt normal, expected. The light was now gone, and she should never seek such fleeting comforts again, because she knew they would always be taken from her.

Bernadette did not return.

When autumn colored the trees and frost covered the ground, Karmin gave birth to a healthy son. Nadia was not permitted to enter the birthing room, because the queen was far too sick to be exposed to anyone other than the masked physicians wearing dark cloaks. Though she was unable to be present with the queen, Nadia gave her silent, conflicted congratulations. She knew Karmin had been determined to birth a son who would inherit the throne, and the queen must have been relieved at her success. Still, it bothered Nadia that the queen risked her life to go through with the birth.

Nadia held the boy but once, when he was four months old.

His body was warm and soft, and she was reminded of her own son. When Karmin's physician saw the look in Nadia's eyes, she hastily retrieved the baby from her. Nadia never held him again.

When the boy turned one, he was already walking and talking, and required more room than the queen's chambers to explore. Nadia enjoyed watching him waddle from a distance. The duke's son was a few months younger than the prince, his hair white as snow like his father's. Nadia knew Ronan, for he had been crawling around the library and down corridors without hardly any supervision for months. But she didn't learn the prince's name until one of the maids was chasing after both of them, calling their names desperately when he caused trouble. When she heard it at last, Nadia faltered, the weight of its meaning striking her sharply:

*Xavelor*—savior, victorious.

A mighty name, befitting the future heir to the throne.

Nadia envied Karmin. She'd been unable to name her own child, wrought with indecision on the birthing bed and almost a year after. She and Lancenel had chosen to let the village select a name for him once his aspirations and personality were more evident.

Karmin's young prince inherited a full head of curly black hair and olive skin. His eyes were dark, like his father's. But he had his mother's round face and full lips. He was a beautiful child.

WHEN XAVELOR WAS NEARLY TWO, the king finally returned.

He did not visit Nadia first—he went directly to his wife and son.

Nadia knew better than to hope he had forgotten her, and yet hope crept in anyway, stubborn and unwelcome. She silently went to the queen's chamber, heart hammering, and pressed her ear to the door. Through the wood, she caught the soft murmur of their voices, the gentle laughter, the intimate whispers...and a pang of longing tightened around her chest.

She couldn't hear their entire conversation, but what she caught sounded surprisingly warm. Perhaps becoming a father had softened the king's heart—though she barely dared to believe it. The rest of the afternoon passed in a haze of anxious self-convincing: she told herself over and over that she would be left in peace, that he would not seek her out.

But when she returned to her bedchamber that night, her stomach tightening with anxiety, the king was already there, waiting.

# XIV

# RUINED

Desperation drove the king to Nadia's bedroom. He had looked upon the child his ailing wife had brought into the world, and in that brief, fragile moment something unfamiliar had stirred in him: a protectiveness, and a sharp, hollow ache he struggled to name.

Yet even that strange emotion could not quiet the pull that brought him here. One child would never be enough. From the moment he first laid claim to Nadia, he had known he wanted an heir who bore her likeness.

Wanted?

No.

*Needed.*

He no longer cared about convincing her to love him. He didn't *require* her love. He only needed her obedience, and that, he could get.

He *would* get it.

When she stepped into her chamber, he was already seated on the edge of her narrow mattress, arms folded. He leveled his gaze on her, watched the way her delicate features tightened, how weariness transformed into open hatred as she took him in. That look—sharp and unguarded—only spurred him further, steeling his resolve to break her will.

She turned to flee, but he was faster. He rose in one fluid motion and caught her by the wrist, his reach spanning the small chamber with ease. She gasped and bent back, too drained to resist his strength.

"Come. Sit." He dragged her with him toward the bed.

She fell in a heap on the mattress, and the king lowered himself calmly beside her. He flexed his fingers, rough from the war he fought over the past year and a half. His body was tired, but never too tired for this moment—the moment he envisioned for so long.

Nadia's voice was a jagged thing. "You're wicked."

So she had grown a backbone after all. Whether it had been forged by her dead lover or tempered by the last year mattered little to him.

Her defiance only sweetened the game.

"I am power," he said. He extended a hand toward her, as though inviting her to take it.

She didn't.

His smile thinned, collapsing into a hard line—

and in the next heartbeat, the back of his hand cracked against her face.

Her body dropped to the bed and her hands shakily went to her bleeding cheek—his ringed fingers had torn through flesh, splitting skin and cracking the bone beneath. Dripping red liquid welled between her fingers, dark, almost black against her pale skin.

He didn't reach to comfort her as he said, "Be grateful. I am offering you one last kindness." He wiped his hand on his tunic, then slipped a marbled disc from the folds of his cloak. Viktor had given it to him—an experimental tincture woven with fairy magic. They had tested it on their foes, slipping it into rations to lull entire battalions into a stupor. It had allowed Azriel's squadron to breach the enemy camp and end the brief war between Midra's outer faction and Arioch.

If only Viktor had crafted the elixir sooner...

Azriel's thumb traced the polished capsule, slow, deliberate. He extended it toward her, voice low and buttery.

"I am giving you a choice," he said, the faintest smirk touching his lips. "Swallow this, and you will remember nothing of tonight. Refuse... and I will see to it that every moment is burned into your mind."

She whipped her head toward him, eyes blazing despite the tears rimming them. Shadows fell over the green of her irises as her voice trembled.

"How *kind* of you," she said.

Azriel laughed, bouncing the elixir in his palm. His patience was growing thin.

Nadia's gaze flicked to the capsule and lingered there. She breathed evenly, chest rising and falling, though each inhale was deep and measured. After a long moment, her eyes met the king's.

"Bastard," she ground out. His smile widened.

Then, with a swift motion, she snatched the capsule from his palm and thrust it into her mouth.

Azriel had been right. What had happened last night was gone from her mind, and she had no desire to call it back. Yet by sunrise, her body protested: a dull ache in her belly, a fire between her thighs, a weight pressing on her chest. She did not need memory to understand what had been done.

He was gone, *thank Aldorin*. And not a single servant waited for her when she awoke.

She went straight to her washroom and vomited into the chamber pot.

Nadia had been alone for many years before meeting Lancenel, but only now did she truly feel isolated. No one was there to support her. The king was her abuser, the queen was bedridden, and her family was gone.

She wrung her hands together until the knuckles whitened, then tipped her head back, hoping for tears her body refused to give. The ache in her throat tightened as memories pressed in around her—shadows of the past that should have been her future—and her knees weakened. She sagged against the wash-basin, its cold rim biting into her spine.

Her body felt foreign beneath her, as though someone had scraped away the person she had been and left only this trembling shell behind. Her skin crawled where his hands had been, a defilement she couldn't remember, but her body did. The king's cruelty lingered like a stain, far beneath the surface, deeper than bone.

She told herself to move. To cleanse. To scrape away the remnants of him until she felt whole again. But her limbs refused her commands. Her fingers dug into the edge of the basin, useless and shaking.

Hatred rose in her like a thick, choking smoke. Hatred for the king who had taken everything from her. And hatred, colder and more insidious, for herself... For the weakness, the helplessness, the inability to reverse time or scream loud enough to stop him.

She stood there, frozen, a single breath away from breaking entirely.

How could Aldorin have let this happen?

She hugged herself and gradually moved to the corner of the washroom, where the least amount of light shone on the stone floor. For as long as she could, she buried her nose in her knees and cried without tears. Her breathing grew ragged, her nose stuffy. But her eyes remained dry, her throat wrecked.

How long did she sit there, uninterrupted by the king or any servants?

She didn't know.

It was as though she was caged again, like in the dungeon. Only this time, she did not wish to leave. Not if it meant she would have to face the king again.

At some point, the elf queen drifted into sleep. She dreamt for what felt like days, her family appearing in fragments of memory. Smiles, their straw-colored hair catching the wind like golden wheat. Lancenel spoke to her, though the words eluded her ears. Still, a lightness bloomed inside her, the kind she had longed for. She missed him, yet *here* he was, alive in her dreams. She never wanted to wake.

She held her baby, cradled his head in her arms. Untouched by damning prophecies, he was hers to keep. She kissed his head and sang him lullabies, the ones she doubted many knew anymore. And she felt his warmth, his innocence, and then—

She was violently shaken awake.

Nadia screamed as her dreams shattered, her eyes snapping open to the cold darkness of her washroom. She didn't know who had disturbed her, and she didn't care. Hands lashed out blindly, swiping at the intruder, fury igniting her limbs. She growled, sharp and animal, snapping like something half-wild.

Warm hands wrapped gently around her wrists, barely containing her.

"Oh, poor, sweet Nadia."

Nadia stopped thrashing, her arms going limp. Then, with a desperate motion, she freed her arms and wrapped them tightly around her visitor, burying her face in the lady's neck.

"Shh." Bernadette stroked the back of Nadia's head. The elf queen sobbed into her friend's shoulder. "I'm sorry I am so late. What happened here? Why are you alone... and so frail, as though you have gone without food for days?"

Nadia tried to steady her breathing. When she met Bernadette's gaze, the understanding she had come to recognize flickered there once more. Could Bernadette already know? Had she chosen to let Nadia speak the truth herself, letting her confess it one careful word at a time?

"Lancenel..." Nadia croaked. She shook her head, tears pricking her crusted eyes. "The king..." She could say no more; the world was already tilting beneath her.

Bernadette nodded gravely, pulling Nadia back to her shoulder.

"I am here now, miss. You can trust me. I will stay with you. You are no longer alone."

Bernadette whispered the words twice more, as though repetition might make them true. "You are no longer alone. You are no longer alone."

Nadia wept—not for comfort, but because she felt nothing at all. Hope, despair, the wish to live, the wish to die... all had vanished.

She was numb.

She was a shell.

And not even Aldorin could fix her.

# XV

# VICTORY

Nadia ate Viktor's elixirs again. Ears rounded, teeth flattened—she looked human, fragile. She followed Bernadette, wore the gowns the lady chose, wandered the grounds, drank tea, and accepted the noblewomen's envious stares without thought.

Nadia's status as royal concubine became official the instant her belly betrayed her condition. She may have birthed a child before, but elven children were slight. This one, of both human and elven blood, was larger, heavier, a constant weight she could not ignore.

During the months she carried her child, King Augustus passed away quietly. His illness had been scarcely known beyond the castle's walls, so the commonfolk were told he had retired to The Valley, a cliff-divided countryside north of Arioch's castle.

Xavelor, almost three, had made a habit of crashing the ladies' tea, diving under skirts and lashing legs with strands of wheat. The ladies adored him, and even Nadia found herself charmed. Mischievous, yes, but utterly irresistible.

As her own child started stirring within her, the memory of the prophecy surged back, cold and suffocating. Panic clawed at her throat—not for herself, but for the soul growing within her.

She didn't yet know if she carried a son or a daughter, only that the air in her chest had turned to lead

One night, she found Bernadette and told her they needed to do everything they could to prevent the destiny awaiting her child. She was wracked with concern, and felt the only thing that could calm her shattered heart was preparation.

"My ring." She twisted the thin silver ornament from her fourth finger and held it out to Bernadette. It had been given to her by the king once the rumor of her status circulated. She was supposed to wear it as a symbol of her loyalty to the king—the kingdom's legendary dragons Myrn and Steil wound together around the band and met at the center, maws open to one another. Almost identical to the queen's wedding band.

Bernadette received the ring, her brow furrowing.

Nadia reached into the pocket of her braies and retrieved a small vial of her blood. It was an insignificant amount, taken from a gash Nadia had made in her arm where the mark of her mating bond had already nearly disappeared. The gauze around the wound was thick enough to hide the freshness of the wound, not yet soaked through with blood.

Bernadette's eyes widened, her mouth going slack. "Miss, is that...?"

Nadia shoved the vial into her friend's hands, covering it with her fingers.

"If there is a smith who can enchant this ring with my blood, can you find them?" Nadia's eyes burned, sharp and unflinching. "My blood, *Aldorin's* blood, will protect my child from whatever magic comes from this unholy union." Bernadette's posture stiffened, but Nadia pressed on, voice tighter now, trembling with a fear she could not hide. "My first child was taken from me. I cannot survive that loss again. I thought I could, but I cannot. This baby is mine just the same."

Bernadette slid the vial and ring into a pocket within her dress and huffed a long breath. "I will have this done immediately," she promised.

Nadia watched her friend go, then re-entered her chambers.

To her relief, no one waited for her. Since Augustus's passing, the king was focused on other issues, and he had already done to her what he'd planned. He had no reason to visit her now.

So she went to bed, the baby in her belly content to rest when she did. Her hands rested under her navel, cradling the unborn child as they dreamed together.

A WEEK before Nadia was predicted to give birth, a group of witches arrived at Azriel's parlor. He remembered them from when they had beckoned him in Arcanvale, voices soft and insistent. They stood in the parlor now, claiming the gods would punish them—and the kingdom—if they were not present for the birth of his second child.

They murmured incantations that made little sense, their wide eyes roaming over the portraits and royal furnishings with great interest.

Their expressions were haunted, as though some heavy knowledge pressed on them, desperate to be freed. Even with the threat they laid easily on his kingdom, Azriel had no desire to see them or hear what they had to say. It was Viktor who advised him to get the meeting over with. Better to endure it once than invite repeated visits.

They settled on velvet cushions at Azriel's command, their ragged clothing stark against the opulence around them. The three witches gripped each other's hands tightly, knuckles white with tension. The king cracked his neck to the side, his mood already soured after a long day spent poring over histories and hearing half-formed tales of the Perri duchy's reputation.

The witches' voices rushed over one another, urgent and disjointed.

"Your Majesty, a prophecy. A *prophecy*, Your Majesty. Two sons, one fate. Who will wait at the seven hells' gates? Spoken once, and written twice, read it now before it's too late." They spoke in disarray, but the words still managed to be clear.

Azriel pressed a thumb to the center of his brow, massaging the tension forming there. A headache throbbed behind his eyes, but he forced his voice flat. "Out with it, then."

One of the witches pulled a crumpled sheet of paper from within her clothing and presented it to the king with a shaky hand.

"Only read it once, aloud, my king. Or a curse shall upon you cling. By the hells' own law, we dare not see, or doom will fall on you and we."

He snatched the crumpled sheet, letting his eyes drift over it without care. Words slid past him, meaningless.

And then—*something*. He grasped the paper again, focusing. The letters lifted, trembling on the page, just out of reach.

"What sorcery is this?" he boomed. "Such trickery is worthy of execution!"

The witches cowered, mumbling high-pitched pleas. Their hands went to their necks, as though to protect them.

"Read it aloud, and you will see. Wait, and witness fate's decree." This time, only one of the witches spoke. Her voice was grave. "Your Majesty, the prophecy names your son. Whether by your wife or your mistress, we know not which one."

Azriel placed the parchment on his desk, anger roiling in his lungs.

"You were foolish to bring such treachery to my awareness," he growled. His eyes flicked to the guards lurking in the shadows, and without another word, they stepped forward, swords sliding silently from their scabbards. "And now," he said, voice low and lethal, "you must pay for your foresight."

Each of the witches' heads fell, squelches of blades cutting through their necks. Silent screams stuck on their lips, their eyes glassy and wide.

"Mages," Azriel said, voice tight.

The cloaked beings appeared next, raising their hands.

The king didn't need to voice his next command.

The witches' bodies were engulfed with bright blue mage fire, and seconds later, there was nothing left of them.

Nothing except the prophecy that burned behind his eyes, warning him of a future heir bent on destroying him and his kingdom. He pictured Xavelor, the brightness in his eyes, the potential behind them. And then he imagined the child Nadia carried, still unborn, still fragile. He reminded himself of the one solid truth ingrained in each Faundor king: magic was meant to *serve* him, not rise against him.

He doubted the trueness of the prophecy...but he could not dismiss it entirely.

And so the seed of paranoia took root.

A king... Crushed by one of two sons. The prophecy was unyielding.

He convinced himself it could not be Xavelor, the son born within wedlock. He was bright-eyed, promising, loyal.

No, the threat had to be the hybrid bastard, forged in hatred, born of spite and shadow.

Azriel swore he would do everything in his power to raise Xavelor into a proper heir, strong and untainted. And when the time came, he would strike down the other son before the prophecy could ever be fulfilled.

Azriel steepled his fingers, his eyebrows pulling together.

"Viktor," he called.

The duke appeared at his side.

"Yes, Your Majesty."

Azriel's eyes flickered. He handed the parchment to Viktor. The duke skimmed it, frowning. Confusion gave way to dawning understanding, and his forehead creased with the knowledge of what was to come.

Azriel folded the parchment and tucked it into his cloak. A wicked smile tugged at his mouth.

"They cannot use this against me," he proclaimed. "I am blessed by Arioch, with not one, but *two* sons. Let them clash over my seat. In their struggle, they will abandon any thought of overthrowing me."

"Nadia will surely protect her own blood," Viktor said.

Azriel waved away his concern, the smile never leaving his face.

"She wishes to die," Azriel said. "And when she does, she will no longer be there to protect him."

"Not if she dies, but *when*, sire?"

"Yes, *when*." Azriel crossed his arms. His grin spread cruelly. He could hardly contain the glory of his hatred, of his power. He looked warmly upon his aide.

"And you'll be the one to do it."

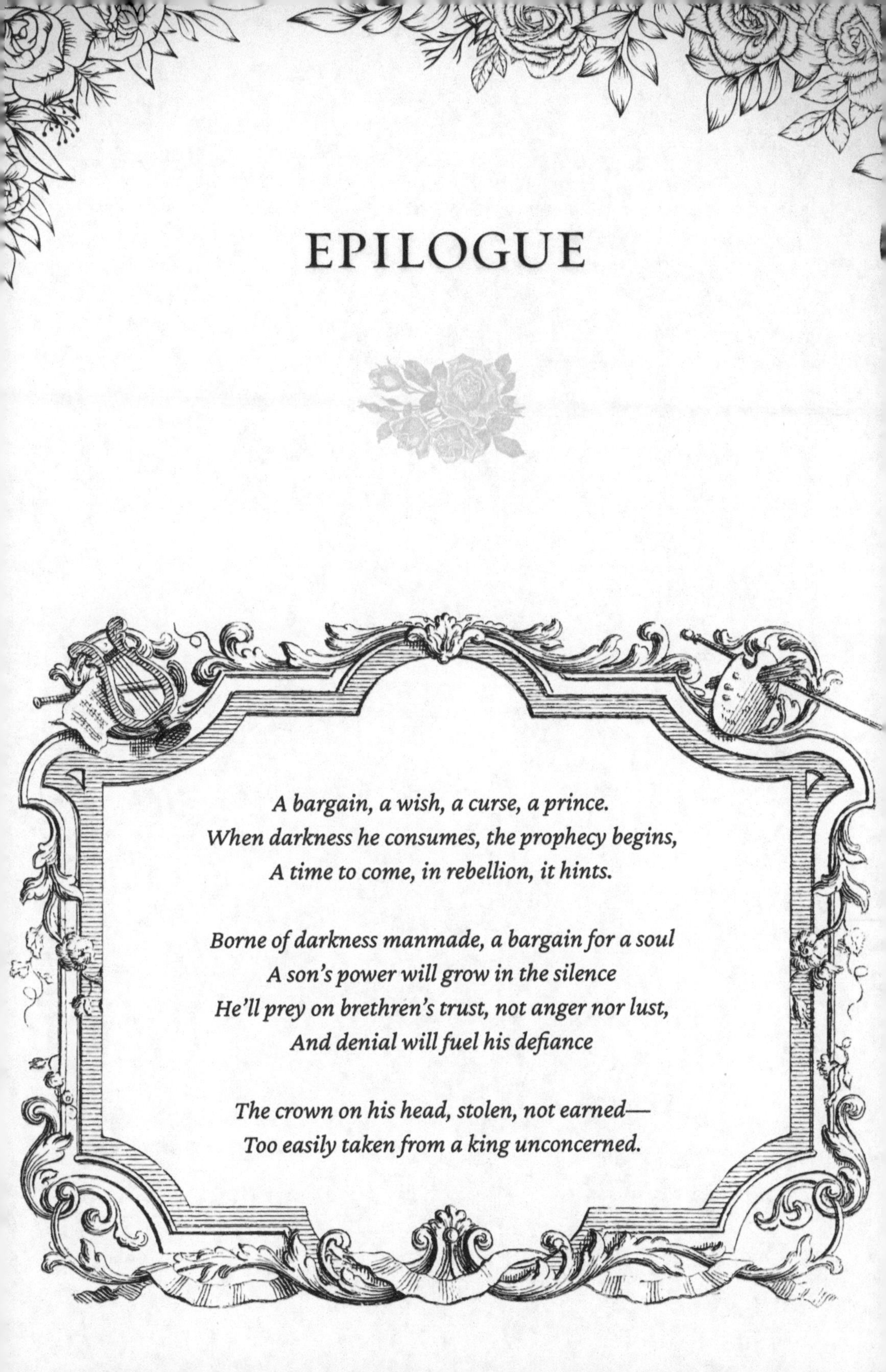

# EPILOGUE

*A bargain, a wish, a curse, a prince.*
*When darkness he consumes, the prophecy begins,*
*A time to come, in rebellion, it hints.*

*Borne of darkness manmade, a bargain for a soul*
*A son's power will grow in the silence*
*He'll prey on brethren's trust, not anger nor lust,*
*And denial will fuel his defiance*

*The crown on his head, stolen, not earned—*
*Too easily taken from a king unconcerned.*

# ACKNOWLEDGMENTS

I could not have completed this prequel novella without the constant support of my husband, August, and my lovely group of writer friends. Your encouragement throughout the start of my author journey and the process with this book mean the world to me.

Of course, I wouldn't have been able to make it this far without the ears I borrowed to listen to my questions and concerns about this prequel and how it leads into book two. My alpha readers were instrumental in giving feedback and positive comments that led this draft to its publication!

I want to thank God, for giving me the spur of motivation I needed each time I carved out time to write, edit, and polish. Frankly, without the women in my small groups and supportive friends at church, I don't think I would've finished this book as quickly as I did. Thank you to all of you, from the bottom of my heart!

And to my little girl, Micaiah: you may not be able to read yet, but I hope that one day, when you do, you can be so proud of your mama. I love you so much, and can't wait for you to dig into books and love them as I do!

I'll see you in book two!

**Kayliani Shi** is an avid reader, artist, and writer. Raised in northern Idaho, she now lives in Michigan with her husband, daughter, two cats, and dog. When not huddled in a blanket writing, Kayliani enjoys taking walks in the sun, visiting local cafés, and listening to her favorite J-ROCK band, Official Hige Dandism. You can find more about Kayliani at kaylianishipr.com.

*The Sinuous Bargain of a Cowardly Prince*
is now an **audiobook**!

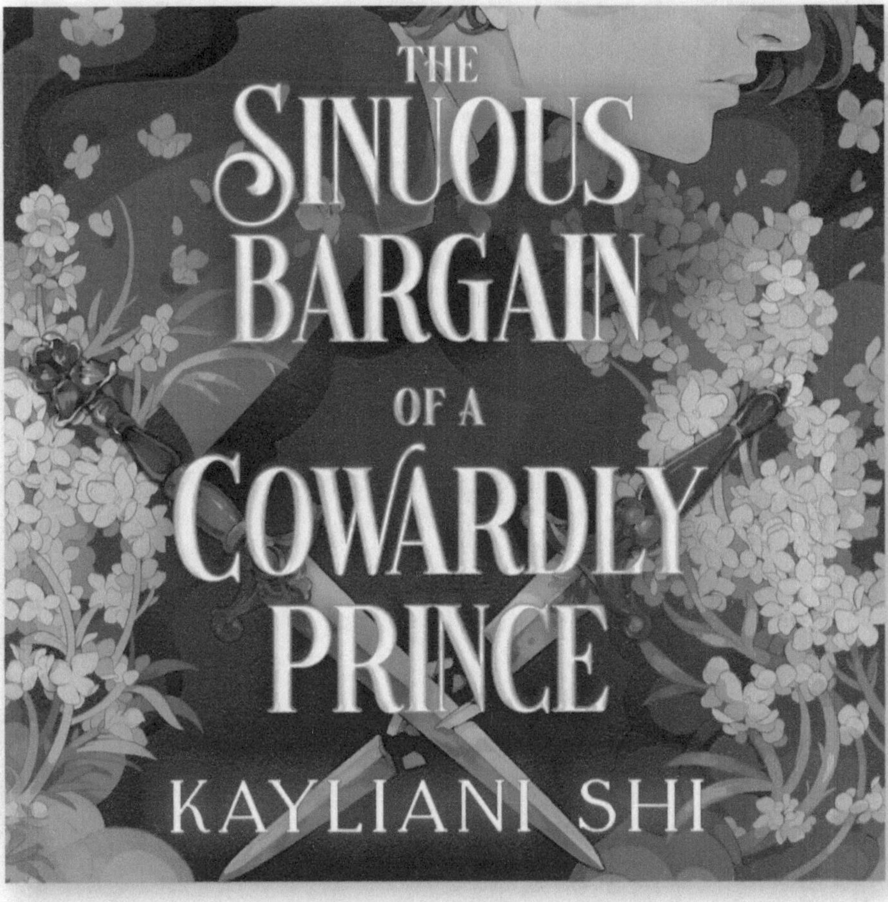

THE
SINUOUS
BARGAIN
OF A
COWARDLY
PRINCE
KAYLIANI SHI

*Listen now on the following streaming apps:*

www.ingramcontent.com/pod-product-compliance
Lightning Source LLC
LaVergne TN
LVHW031343150826
845673LV00009B/2836